FERAL HEAT

SHIFTERS UNBOUND
BOOK 5.5

JENNIFER ASHLEY

JA / AG PUBLISHING

Feral Heat

Shifters Unbound Book 5.5

Copyright © 2013 by Jennifer Ashley

This book is a work of fiction. The names, characters, places, and incidents are products of the writer's imagination or have been used fictitiously and are not to be construed as real. Any resemblance to persons, living or dead, actual events, locales or organizations is entirely coincidental.

All Rights are Reserved. No part of this book may be used or reproduced in any manner whatsoever without written permission from the author. Nor is this book to be used to train AI databases.

Cover design by Kim Killion

CHAPTER ONE

The fight club had moved since Jace Warden had last visited the Austin Shiftertown. The Shifters used to meet for their forbidden bouts in an abandoned hay barn nestled into folds of a hill, but the land had been purchased, and a developer had built over it.

On his borrowed Harley, Jace turned from the discreet plane that had flown him this far and headed down a highway that led to drier country away from the river. The world had darkened while he'd flown east from Nevada to land at an airfield that had supposedly been closed.

Dylan Morrissey, the Austin Shiftertown liaison, had left a message for Jace to meet him at the fight club, and he'd also left the bike for Jace's transportation.

Tired and hot, and having hauled himself halfway across the country at Dylan's request, the last thing Jace wanted to do was to ride out to the fight club. But Dylan had summoned him to work on the problem of getting the Collars off Shifters once and for all, and had extended his hospitality. So Jace hid his irritation, thanked the humans who'd helped him get this far, and mounted the motorcycle.

Jace turned off where the directions had instructed, the paved road quickly turning to dirt, the bike bouncing and skidding over gravel and through ruts. The road grew narrower and narrower, until it petered to nothing. Jace continued down a short hill and around a bend, and found the Shifter fight club behind a slight rise that hid it from the road.

He smelled it long before he saw the electric lanterns, fire dancing in garbage cans, and flashlights. Anything that could be quickly doused was being used to illuminate the scene.

Jace would have known it was a place of Shifters, even in the pitch-dark. Shifters working off adrenaline rushes and fighting instincts had a certain interesting—and pungent—odor.

Jace killed the engine of the bike, parking it among the pack of motorcycles, pickups, and smaller cars. He hung the helmet from the seat and made sure his backpack was well stashed in the saddlebag before he approached the fight area. He wasn't worried about Shifters stealing his change of clothes and toothbrush—Shifters didn't steal from one another, because a simple snatch could end up in a fight to the death. Possessions were territory, and territory was respected. But humans also came to the fight clubs, and some liked to abscond with things.

The new fighting arena was a broad slab of concrete about a hundred feet long and just as wide. Probably an old building or an event area of some kind, abandoned by its owners when money ran out. Everything had been pulled away except the slab.

Rings were outlined by concrete blocks, and firelight flickered wildly, making it a scene from hell, complete with demons. But the demons were only Shifters having fun and working off steam. Those not fighting were cheering, drinking beer, or finding hook-ups—human or Shifter—and sneaking into the darkness to work off steam a different way.

Jace made his way around cars—a few of them being used for liaisons—and toward the firelight. He didn't worry about locating Dylan in the chaos, because Dylan, a Feline Shifter who was mostly lion, always made himself known.

What Jace didn't expect was the wolf who sprang out of the shadows in a deserted stretch of the parking area and landed on Jace full force.

Jace swung around with the impact, hands coming up to dig into the wolf's fur and throw him down. The Lupine landed in the dust, his Collar sparking and sizzling. The Collar's shocks didn't slow the wolf much, because he rolled to his feet and charged Jace again.

Jace didn't know who the hell the wolf was. Not that he had much of a chance of identification as the Lupine landed on Jace again, his Collar's sparks burning Jace's skin. The wolf went for Jace's throat, and Jace's hands turned to leopard's paws to rake across the wolf's face. The wolf took the blow, landed on his feet, shook himself, and sprang again.

Jace's Collar hadn't shocked him yet, but he felt the build-up. Collars were made to spike pain into Shifters as soon as they became seriously violent, but Jace had learned techniques to fool the Collar and keep it dormant. It was tough to do, however, especially when he was taken by surprise. Jace had to focus in order to keep the Collar quiet, and right now he was busy trying to keep this bloody Lupine from killing him.

Jace whacked the wolf aside again, spinning around as he shed his denim jacket and half shifted to his wildcat. His shirt split, jeans falling as his back legs elongated into powerful feline haunches. He emerged from his shredding clothes as a fully formed snow leopard—creamy fur, black spots, ice blue eyes—and thoroughly pissed off.

Jace went for the wolf. The wolf was bigger, almost twice Jace's bulk, but leopards hadn't made it to the top of the wildcat pyramid because of size. Leopards might be among the smaller big cats, but they were swift, agile, and smart, and they didn't take shit from anyone.

This wolf wanted to give him shit, though. He came at Jace again, fur up, his canine jowls frothing, his golden eyes filled with rage. The scent that hit Jace reeked of challenge. This was a wolf who wanted to move up in rank, never mind that Jace was a different species and not even from this Shiftertown. Dominance challenges weren't allowed inside the ring at the fight club. One of the biggest rules was that fights were for recreation and showing off— that, and no killing. Outside the ring was a different story.

Jace got ready to teach him a lesson.

As he drew back to renew his attack, another wolf sprang from the parking lot and hurled itself at the first wolf. A female, Jace scented, one he hadn't met before.

She wasn't rushing to defend the wolf, however. She

attacked the Lupine in fury, teeth bared, near madness in her eyes.

The first Lupine swung to meet her, and the two went down in an explosion of fur and snarls. Jace sat back to catch his breath, surprised. The two wolves were evenly matched, the male a bit larger than the female, but the female was plenty strong and agile. Probably dominant to the male too.

Jace let the female get her first anger out of her system, then he waded back in to rescue his rescuer.

The male Lupine had the she-wolf on the ground by now. He pinned the female with one big paw, snarling as he turned to Jace.

Jace gave him a warning growl. The growl said that, up until now, Jace had been holding back, that Jace was dominant in his pride, his clan, and his Shiftertown, and the wolf might want to think about it before continuing the fight.

The Lupine ignored the warning and went for the kill. Jace met him head-on, his lithe body and fast paws taking the wolf down to the ground before the Lupine could use his superior weight to his advantage.

The she-wolf rose behind the male, landed on the wolf's back, and sank her teeth into his neck. Her Collar was sparking frantically, and she got hit by the arcs from the other wolf's Collar, but she kept biting.

Jace drew back his paw and whacked the male wolf across the throat. The wolf spun with the blow, knocking the female loose. The male Lupine rolled across the dust and dying grass a long way before he was able to stop. He righted himself but stayed down on his belly, panting hard, conceding the fight.

Jace walked to him with a stiff-legged Feline stalk. When he reached the Lupine, he lowered his head to the wolf's eye level and growled again. *Stay the fuck down.*

Whether or not the Lupine understood Feline rumbles and body language, Jace's glare must have gotten the message across. The wolf snarled, teeth bared, but he plastered his ears flat on his head and didn't move.

Jace turned back to the she-wolf. She lay limply on the grass, and Jace went to her, giving her a cat's lick across her face. She growled softly, and Jace licked her again, feeling a need to thank and reassure her.

The need didn't leave him when he shifted back to human. He stroked her head, liking the wiry fur of her wolf.

The female wolf looked up at him in a wash of confusion. She was a gray wolf, with gray eyes. She breathed in Jace's scent, wrinkling her nose, clearly wondering who he was.

Jace gave her head another stroke, wishing she'd turn back to human so he could talk to her. She'd run to his rescue, a Lupine taking the side of a Feline, and Jace wanted to know why.

The she-wolf remained wolf, still growling softly. Jace touched her head one last time and walked back to the male wolf. "New way of greeting guests in Shiftertown?" he asked. "Let me introduce myself. I'm Jace Warden. A guest of Dylan's."

Jace knew he didn't need to explain that his own father was leader of another Shiftertown. The fact that

Dylan sanctioned Jace's visit should be enough for this wolf.

The wolf morphed into his human form, a man with short black hair and light gray eyes. "Hey, I saw a strange Feline trying to sneak into the fight club when he wasn't invited, and when no one but regulars are supposed to know about the new place. What did you expect?"

"So you were defending all the Shifters here?" Jace asked with evident skepticism. "Commendable."

"Ask that crazy bitch what *she* was doing," the Lupine said, scowling at the she-wolf. "Nurturing females, my ass. She's all spit and vinegar."

"Let me guess." Jace felt mirth. "She turned down your mate-claim."

The Lupine gave Jace an incredulous look. "I wouldn't mate-claim *her*. Not if she were the last female in Shiftertown. She's out of her mind. You can never tell what she's going to do." The man made a broad gesture in her direction. "You saw her."

"I thought it was nice of her to help me out."

"Nah, she saw a fight, it sparked her loony side, and she dove in. Look at her. She's not even sure what happened."

Jace turned his gaze to the she-wolf again and saw that the man was right. She watched Jace and the Lupine, trembling but trying to hide it with a growl and a glare. Jace saw fear in her eyes along with deep anger—a woman hurting from something and not wanting anyone else to know it.

"I keep trying to tell Liam she should be put down," the Lupine said. "She's a danger to the rest of us."

The she-wolf snarled again. Scent and body language told Jace what he needed to know—the female was dominant but of a different clan than the male wolf, and the male was aggressive, cocky, and hated to be bested. The male wolf would be dominant in his clan as well. Jace outranked both of them, though.

Jace looked into the other man's eyes. "Why don't you shut your hole, get dressed, and go the hell home? You're too unstable to be here tonight."

The man tried to meet Jace's gaze. He did pretty well, but in the end had to slide his eyes sideways. "What, you want some privacy with her? Don't say I didn't warn you."

"Just go," Jace said.

The wolf snorted. "Whatever." He climbed to his feet and strolled away, not worried that he was naked.

The fight hadn't attracted any attention. A sudden roar of voices within the arena told Jace why—there must be an intense match going down. The human voices were accompanied by roars and growls, since half the watchers would be in animal form.

Jace retrieved his torn clothing, grunting in irritation. He'd only brought two changes of clothes, thinking he wouldn't be in Austin that long.

The jeans had escaped the worst of the shredding, and he pulled them on, the ripped seams stretching as he crouched down to look at the she-wolf again.

"You all right?" he asked her. "Who was that asshole?"

The disgust in his question reached past the feral fear in her eyes. He saw clarity return, and then the wolf shifted into a female with a lush, lovely body, close-cut wheat-colored hair, and large gray eyes.

She remained in a crouch, covering herself, but Jace's gaze traced the curve of her ample breasts, his natural need rising. She'd be worth sneaking off into the darkness with, maybe having a bounce with in the bed of a pickup.

No, she'd be worth more than that. This wasn't a lady Jace would use to relieve horniness and then forget. Not with that gorgeous gaze pinning him flat.

"His name's Broderick," she said in a voice Jace wanted to embrace. "He usually wins Asshole of the Month around here."

"No doubt. What did you jump in for? He's right about one thing—it was a crazy thing to do. Two males with their blood up could have hurt you."

"I saw him besting you. No one deserves to be pounded by Broderick for no reason."

"He wasn't besting me," Jace said, giving her a grin. "I had him. And then he started kicking *your* ass."

She frowned. "Oh, please. I was a few bites away from making him crawl away whimpering."

As Jace hoped, his needling made her irritation erase her fear and pain. "Not to mention, your Collar was going off," Jace said. "Are you sure you're all right?"

He placed his hand on the side of her neck, over the Collar in question. Ordinarily, Jace wouldn't touch uninvited, especially not cross-species, but something in this woman cried out to him. She needed soothing.

Her eyes widened a little, but she didn't jerk away. "What about you? Your Collar *didn't* go off. You can dampen its effect, can't you? Like Liam does?"

Jace let his fingers caress her neck as he chose his words. "That's not supposed to be common knowledge. Need-to-know basis."

"Maybe I need to know. Dylan's trying to teach me, but I can't do it yet."

"In that case, I'll give you some pointers." Jace traced her Collar to the front, pausing when his fingers rested on its Celtic cross lying against her throat. "But I'd better find Dylan and tell him I'm here before the payback for controlling my Collar hits me."

"Dylan's fighting right now," the woman said. "His bouts are always popular. But short. He should be done soon."

Jace placed his hand on hers. He wanted to keep touching this woman for some reason, as though breaking contact with her would lessen him somehow. "Come with me. We'll watch him win together."

"No." The woman started to rise, and Jace unfolded himself and helped her to her feet. She didn't hide herself anymore, a Shifter woman unembarrassed by her body. "I have to go. Are you Jace? You've been to Shiftertown before, haven't you?"

"Yeah, but why haven't I met you?" Jace still didn't want to release her hand. "I've made lots of trips out here, but I don't remember seeing you."

"I've been ... sick," she said. "I'm Deni. Deni Rowe."

Deni watched him anxiously, as though gauging his reaction to the name. "Ellison Rowe's sister?" Jace asked.

"Yes." Deni still peered at him, waiting.

Jace tightened his hand on hers. "Why do you have to go? Stay with me and watch Dylan kick ass. You can keep other Lupines from jumping me."

Deni didn't smile. She glanced at the arena and the

mass of figures there, and Jace scented her nervousness. "I can't. Sometimes the fighting ..."

"Calls to the feral in you? Makes you lose control?"

She gave him a startled look. "How did you know that?"

"Because I saw your eyes when you attacked Broderick. You didn't dive into the fight only to rescue me. You did it because watching made you want to fight too. I was like that during my Transition." Jace caressed the hand he hadn't released. "All you have to do is hold on to someone. The touch will calm you and keep you tethered."

Another startled look. "That doesn't work. Even my cubs ..."

"Bet me," Jace said. "You hang on to a dominant, and he takes the heat and cools you down. Works. That's what dominants are for."

A spark of pride returned to Deni's eyes. "And you're saying you're dominant to me?"

"Yep. It's obvious. You outrank Broderick—I bet you outrank a lot of wolves—but you're not dominant to this Feline." He touched his chest.

She gave him a half smile. "And you're not full of yourself about that."

"Just stating facts." Jace did *not* want to let go of her hand. "Let's find your clothes and go. Unless you want to watch as wolf."

Deni sent him another haughty look that made her eyes beautiful, but she didn't pull away. "I'll find my clothes."

"Good."

Jace left his shredded shirt behind—why bother with it?—but caught up his jacket and followed her into the darkness, her hand on his like a lifeline. A warm, sweet lifeline. He definitely wanted to know this Lupine woman better.

———

Deni's heart beat swiftly as she pulled on the sarong she'd thrown off to rush into the fight with Broderick. Broderick's scent of arrogance had enraged her, and she'd wanted to pummel him for jumping the other Shifter without challenge.

Then she'd felt her memory slide away, the feral thing inside her taking over. She shivered. Her wildness hadn't receded until Jace had smacked the wolf down himself, and Deni had fallen away from the fight.

Jace hadn't then turned around and kicked her butt, as he'd had a right to for interfering. Instead he'd touched her, licked her with his strange Feline sandpapery tongue, then held her hand after she'd changed back to human.

Deni was still shaky as they entered the fight club's main area. Jace kept hold of her hand. It was a big hand, warm but callused, his grip strong. He was a fighter, a warrior.

If Deni remembered right, Jace Warden was the son of Eric Warden, leader of the Las Vegas Shiftertown. Jace was third in command there, the second in command being Eric's sister. Jace would be in the most dominant Feline clan of his Shiftertown, and in the most dominant Feline pride of that clan. The top of the top.

Alphas usually bugged Deni, because they could be

arrogant shits, but only concern and protection flowed from Jace. An alpha interested in taking care of others. What a concept.

The biggest crowd gathered around the central ring—the other two rings were empty. From throats, beast and human, came wild cries, delight in whoever was winning, groaning from those foolish enough not to back Dylan.

Jace moved through the throng to the ring. Shifters moved aside for him, most without noticing they did so. Instinct, Deni guessed—sensing that they should get out of Jace's way before he made it an order.

A large man stood at the perimeter of the ring, arms folded, the Sword of the Guardian on his back. Deni always felt a frisson of dread when she saw the sword, whose purpose was to be driven through the hearts of dead or dying Shifters. The sword pierced the heart, and the Shifter turned to dust, his or her soul following the pathway to the Summerland.

The sword shimmered a little in the flickering light. Other Shifters gave the Guardian a wide berth, also uncomfortable with him. Kind of hard on Sean, Deni always thought, but Sean had been much less haunted since he'd taken a mate.

A human woman stood next to Sean—not his mate. She was the scrappy woman who'd tied herself to Ronan, a Kodiak bear, who was even now in the ring, fighting Dylan. The woman—Elizabeth—danced on top of the cement blocks, cheering for Ronan at the top of her lungs.

Sean would be standing as second for Dylan, his father. A second's job was to make sure that no one interfered with the fight and that the other side didn't cheat.

Dylan and Ronan would go for a fair, straight fight, but other Shifters could be cunning. The seconds were there for a reason.

Dylan was the black-maned lion snarling in the middle of the ring, his paws moving lightning fast as he battled the bigger bulk of the Kodiak. Ronan was fully shifted to bear, his ruff standing up, his eyes alight with fighting fury. Ronan's Collar sparked deep into his fur, but Dylan's was quiet.

"Unfair advantage," Jace said into Deni's ear. "Dylan knows how to keep his Collar from going off."

Deni had to turn her head and stand on tiptoe to answer into Jace's ear. His hand in hers was warm, and she leaned close. "That's why he only fights the strongest: Ronan, or Spike, who's the champion. Sometimes Dylan lets his Collar go off on purpose, to keep things interesting."

"But he usually wins anyway," Jace finished.

He had a rumbling baritone that tickled inside her ear, his hot breath making Deni tingle even more. She squeezed his fingers a little, and was rewarded with an answering squeeze.

Ronan roared. His Collar was sparking, his mate yelling her encouragement, but Deni saw her worry. These matches weren't to the death, but Shifters could be badly hurt in them.

Deni could scent and sense Elizabeth's excitement tinged with fear. She also caught Sean's tenseness as he watched his father battle. If something went wrong, if one of the Shifters was hurt so much the Guardian was needed,

Sean would have to plunge his sword into the heart of either his father or his close friend.

Deni caught his sorrow—Sean had had to send one of his brothers to dust a dozen years ago—which laced through the sorrow in her own heart. Deni wished her cubs were here, her boys, but they were working at their jobs in the city, earning what little money Shifters were allowed to.

Dylan backed away from Ronan's onslaught, ears flat on his head. He didn't roar—Dylan's roar could shake apart the town—but his growls filled the space.

The sound caught in Deni's nerves, calling to the feral inside her. All Shifters had the instinct to throw off any polish of civilization, to revert to their wild forms, to return to the time when they'd been bred to fight and hunt. Even after a thousand and more years, Shifters retained the same basic instincts—fight or be killed, hunt or be hunted.

Shifters had come up with strict rules, made to tame their inner beasts. To keep themselves from tearing each other apart after they'd fought free of their Fae masters, Shifters had agreed to certain rituals that must be performed in regard to mating, fighting, and even death. Take those away, and they were simply animals who could make themselves look human.

Deni's motorcycle accident last year had robbed her of the veneer of calm Shifters strived to learn. The wreck must have jarred something loose in Deni's brain, because she'd been fighting her instincts ever since, often losing. Knowing the bastard who'd run her down was dead had helped her begin to heal, but she wasn't there yet.

In the midst of the growls, snarls, roars, and cheers,

with the scent of blood and sweat pouring from the ring, Deni's thoughts began to tangle. Her scent sense heightened, bringing in the excitement of the Shifters, the bloodlust in Dylan, the singed-fur smell from the sparking Collars, the strong male scent of Jace Warden next to her.

She probably would have been all right with Jace's calming hand in hers, if the fighting Shifters had been anyone else, but Dylan had a powerful Shifter presence. Being alpha didn't simply mean winning fights and scaring Shifters into submission. It was an indefinable something about the Shifter—scent, timbre of voice, subtle compulsion to follow this male. In animal form, it was more apparent, and Dylan was broadcasting his force loud and clear.

Since the accident, Deni had been able to use her animal senses fully in her human form. All Shifters retained some of their superior senses of hearing, scenting, and tracking ability when human, but they were muted, distant, able to be pushed aside so the Shifter could live as human without going crazy.

Not so for Deni. She had to constantly fight herself not to shift, attack, or even kill when she was confused, afraid, or angry. *Going feral* was the term. Her Collar tried to shock sense into her, but that only resulted in more pain, more confusion, more anger.

Deni smelled Dylan's fighting blood, which announced to everyone there he was far stronger and meaner than the giant bear he battled. Ronan continued swinging his enormous paws, landing blows on the smaller lion. Dylan's lithe body moved and flowed with the hits that would have crushed any Shifter who'd stood still and taken them. Dylan's lion's paws moved in a flurry, batting back the bear with the swift, manic strength of a cat.

Deni's wolf howled to life. She wanted to leap into the ring, rush to Dylan's side, and help him fight. He was her alpha—he'd been leader of all Shifters for a long time before conceding his position to his son. Ronan was lesser than Deni, and he dared to confront Dylan. Now Ronan must pay.

Deni clenched her free hand into a fist, jaw so tight it ached. She shouldn't be here—she should have gone home and not let the compelling Jace talk her into watching the battle. She now wanted more than anything to break all the rules of the fight club and run into the ring. Ronan would knock her senseless before he could stop himself, but her wolf didn't care. The bear needed to go down.

Deni started to growl, the sound rising in her throat. Her Collar snapped a spark into her, but she didn't stop. She *couldn't* stop. And that terrified her most of all.

"Hey," a deep voice in her ear rumbled. "Hold it together."

Jace. His warmth covered her side, his stern command reaching her inner beast and stilling the need to shift. Deni realized her fingers had already changed to wolf claws, and fur ran from her head down her back, which was bared by the sarong.

Jace didn't let go of her hand, though she felt her claws pierce his skin. He ran his other hand, warm and broad-palmed, up and down her back, which returned to human smoothness.

"Want to go?" he asked her.

Deni nodded. She couldn't see much anymore—the

fires and lanterns blurred into one whirling light, the shouts and growls blending into a mass of animal sound.

Jace tugged her away, again becoming the lifeline that drew her through the crowd. In the howling, swirling madness, Jace was a constant, his warmth pulling her onward.

He took her into the parking lot, turning her away from the lights. Once the cool night air touched her, darkness erasing the maddening lights, Deni drew a long breath. Her fur and claws receded, leaving her on her human feet, shaking.

"I shouldn't have done that," Jace was saying as they threaded their way through parked vehicles. She heard his voice but didn't pay much attention to the words. "I shouldn't have taken you in there. I didn't realize it was that bad."

"It's bad," Deni said, nodding. She wasn't concentrating on her words either. "I should have stayed home tonight, but I needed ..." She shivered. "I don't know what I needed."

Not true. Deni had needed escape, life, not hiding in the dark. Her sons had gone to work, Ellison had taken his mate, Maria, out for dinner and probably sex, and the rest of Shiftertown had emptied to attend the fight club. Sit at home and mope or go out and be with her friends and neighbors? She'd been tired of moping, so here she was.

Deni's uncontrolled instincts were punishing her now. Jace had known to take her out of there before she did something stupid, but the wildness in her didn't calm. It needed release.

Deni's wolf needed to fight, to hunt, to kill. Robbed of that, the she-wolf in her wanted the nearest thing to it.

She swung to Jace, his scent filling her, his strength calling to her. He was solid, strong, male, and he was here with her in the dark. She couldn't have stopped herself even if she'd wanted to.

Deni slammed both hands to Jace's chest. He caught her with a strong grip but fell against the side of a pickup, carrying her back with him. He had a musky male scent, a little wild, like the woods on a moonlit night. The moon was high and full tonight, always irresistible to a wolf.

Jace's eyes were unusual, jade green, the color heightened by his tanned face and brown black hair he'd buzzed short. He was large too, but agile and athletic.

He watched her, not shoving her away, not angry. Just watching.

Another surge of sound came from the arena, human and animal crying out for blood. Deni snarled, pinned Jace against the truck, and kissed him hard on the mouth.

CHAPTER TWO

J ace found himself with his arms full of gorgeous woman. A *hungry* gorgeous woman. Her kiss pushed him flat against the truck, the ridges of its door digging into his back.

Against his front, he felt nothing but soft woman—breasts, hands, thighs. Deni's mouth was all over his, lips seeking, tongue swiping into his mouth, giving him a taste of spice and wildness.

Jace told himself to push her away, but he cupped her waist and ended up dragging her closer. Another roar came from the arena, galvanizing her, winding up Jace's heat in response.

The sarong bared much of her flesh—the garment clasped at one shoulder and wrapped her hips, leaving Deni's neck, arms, and most of her back bare. Her warm skin was silken under Jace's fingers, curves lush. A full-bodied Shifter woman.

Deni was tall, as Shifter women were, but Jace was

taller. He scooped her into him, liking how she fit against him. Her buttocks were a handful, her breasts the best cushions.

He opened his mouth to hers, welcoming her greedy kisses. She was hot in his arms, she smelled good, and her hair was silken against his skin.

It was exciting, pulling a woman he'd just met into his arms, the two of them wound up from the fighting, wanting to relieve themselves in the shadows with fervent, hard sex. Her body rubbed his hard-on, tingling raw pleasure through him. Some Shifters were already scratching their itches tonight in this parking lot, with humans or other Shifters. By the sounds and scents, they were at it in cars or in the shadows beyond. Frantic, basic coupling.

Deni groped for the button of his jeans, fingers sliding along the zipper. In a few seconds, she'd have his hot cock in her hands, and he'd be done for.

"Not here," Jace managed to say. He had just enough presence of mind to not want to be caught banging Ellison Rowe's sister up against the side of a Shifter's pickup. A few steps and they'd be in deep shadow, on hard Texas earth.

Deni nodded, her eyes the light gray of her wolf. Jace swung her off her feet and ran with her beyond the circle of light.

He didn't bother trying to find a soft place to lie down in the darkness. Jace could hold the both of them up—he was plenty strong. One tug of strings and the sarong fell, baring her to him. Jace buried his nose in her neck as he nipped her flesh. He loved how she smelled. Feminine, strong, beautiful.

Deni managed to get his jeans open. Jace let them slither down his legs, then his underwear followed. He lifted her, cradling her hips, and she slid straight onto him.

Her eyes widened. Beautiful silver white eyes, moonlight eyes. Jace caught her head with one hand, loving the feel of her hair against his fingers, and he kissed her.

Hot, amazing woman wrapped around him, as hungry as he was. Jace was deep inside her, the penetration satisfying, filling him up as much as he filled her.

Deni moaned a little against his mouth. Jace released her from the kiss, but he wanted to go on kissing her, her mouth hot. Goddess, how lucky was he that she'd run to join in his fight?

Jace thrust what little he could, lifting her with hands under her buttocks and lowering her onto him again in small, swift jerks. They were both making noises now, and not being quiet. Anyone passing would know two Shifters were finding relief out here in the dark.

This was raw, rough sex. No finesse, no romance. Just a man and a woman doing what the Goddess had made them to do. Come together, join, mate, create.

"Jace."

Deni cried his name, then her head went back, passion making her incoherent. Jace held on to her, taking their combined weight on his planted feet, rocking to seek more and more of her.

He gathered her hard against him, feeling his seed build in its need to reach her. Shifters wanted more than anything to make more Shifters, and Jace's body knew it. Instinct, desire, whatever he wanted to call it. It took over, and he couldn't fight it.

"Son of a *bitch*," he whispered as his climax hit him, harder than any he'd had in his life. He felt his seed go and felt her take it, heard his own shouts drowned in hers and another, final victory roar from the arena.

Jace shuddered, whatever the hell he said lost to the night. Deni clung to him, her gasps of pleasure not muffled. She hung on to him until the last thrust, and then Jace simply held her, wondering that he'd found something so beautiful so unexpectedly.

His body was still crazed with need. He felt his cock rise again, not that it had deflated much.

Oh, hell no. Jace was crawling with heat, desire rampaging through his body. He thought he'd be sated with a quick coupling—that both of them would be sated.

But the Shifter in him had other ideas. *Mate. Take. Mine.* "Son of a bitch," he whispered again.

This was *not* the time for mating frenzy—that basic Shifter need to take a mate someplace safe where they could screw for days. And days. Weeks, even months if need be. Not to come out until they were both half-starved and exhausted, and the female was plump with cubs.

Shifters could follow their rituals, ceremonies, laws, protocol—whatever they called it this century—but the truth was that the mating frenzy could still grab them by the balls at any time and not let them go.

The woman in Jace's arms had awakened his frenzy as no other female had before. This was crazy. Jace had only just met her—he hadn't known her more than an hour.

The mating frenzy didn't care.

With effort, Jace made himself loosen his hold on her. At least he could give Deni the chance to run.

Then I can hunt her, the leopard in him said with glee. *Chase her. Catch her. Make her mine.*

He was so screwed.

Deni gasped. Jace hadn't been able to look away from her, her light hair and face a pale smudge in the darkness, but now her eyes were round with fear as she gazed off at something behind him. Jace turned his head to see what had caught her worry, and his own breath constricted.

Across the flat plain behind the arena, about a mile away Jace would guess, came lights. Flashing lights—red and blue—and the white pulses of headlights. A ton of them, sirens blaring, all heading toward the arena.

———

"Shit." Jace snarled and grabbed at his jeans, zipping them as Deni groped for her fallen sarong. She wrapped the cloth around herself, fastening it quickly, her heart pounding.

Human police poured toward them, racing for the Shifters' very illegal fight club. Not good. Not good at all.

Even as Jace pulled on his denim jacket and started at a run for the arena, Deni following, her body thrummed with elation. For a year now, she'd been walking around in a half-aware state, but at this moment, in spite of the imminent danger, she was *alive*.

She was a little embarrassed she'd grabbed Jace like that, barely able to control her mating urge, but dear God and Goddess, he'd taken her in a storm. Deni wasn't a stranger to casual sex—Shifters often needed to burn off steam—but this encounter went beyond in intensity anything she'd experienced before.

Deni couldn't stop watching Jace's lithe body as he ran, the grace of his wildcat evident even in his human form. He smelled of the road, of dust, of himself, and now of what they'd done together. The combination made Deni want to catch him, throw him down, and fling herself on top of him. She was shameless, but he was beautiful, virile, and strong, and Deni wanted him with a mindlessness that unnerved her. Even the string of lights and sirens couldn't dampen her need.

Deni sprinted into the arena alongside Jace to find that Dylan's match had finished, though the noise hadn't much lessened. Ronan was sitting heavily on a bench, human again, breathing hard and looking rueful. His mate was wiping his naked body with a towel, giving him it's-all-right-I-still-love-you caresses.

Dylan took his triumph in stride, but quietly, without gloating. His mate, on the other hand, a tall blonde named Glory, watched Dylan admiringly, her gaze roving Dylan's honed body. She opened her mouth, probably to boast that her mate was undefeatable, but Jace's voice cut over the din.

"Cops!" he boomed. "Coming. *Now!*"

The Shifters who'd been celebrating, or grumbling about Ronan's loss, came alert. Shifters stopped, jerked around, stared at Jace or gazed beyond him. Stillness, silence, and animal wariness took over, erasing anything human about them.

Then one of the Shifters yelled, "Go to ground!" and the arena erupted again into noise.

"No!" Jace bellowed over them all. "*Stop!*"

The power of his voice sent a hush rippling across the Shifters again. Jace had the compelling presence of a leader, Deni noted with admiration, the ability to make others stand still and listen, no matter how dire the situation.

Jace had his hands up. "If we run, they chase," he said, his words carrying across the arena. "The slowest will be caught."

The Shifters' unease didn't lessen, Deni saw, and the smell of fear was high. They wanted to flee, and damn the consequences.

"The lad's right," Dylan said. In spite of his bruised and abraded body, he stood upright, his blue eyes hot. "No one gets taken. We stand."

"Then we all get arrested," someone else shouted.

No one moved, though. They wouldn't ignore Dylan.

"No, we won't," Deni said. She stepped up onto one of the cement blocks, using Jace's shoulder to steady herself. "They're going to find us—no time to get away. But *we* can decide what they find. I have an idea."

In a few brief sentences, Deni outlined what she had in mind. The humans looked bewildered, but Shifter faces began to relax, smiles starting to take the place of fear.

"You're cunning, sweetheart," Jace said. His hand on her back was warm as he slanted her a grin. "Anything you're not good at?"

Deni went hot all over, her face flaming as his eyes sparkled. She wasn't sure what the consequences would be of her crazed mating in the parking lot with Jace, but the look he was giving her made her decide that losing control had been worth it.

"You heard her," Dylan said. "This is what we do."

Shifters broke off, organizing themselves as only Shifters could when the need was upon them. The police cars and lights came nearer, sirens cutting the air. Deni still sensed deep fear, the humans barely containing it, the Shifters striving to suppress it.

The waves of panic caught her, jarring Deni's already-heightened nerves. The wolf in her growled, wanting to shift, to confront her enemies and make them run. To chase them if need be and bring them down.

Deni clenched her hands, shuddering, a bead of sweat running down her back. Damn it. If she lost it now, she'd condemn them all.

A comforting touch warmed her shoulder. "Easy," Jace said, his breath in her ear.

He was leaning close, his body heat wrapping around her, his scent relaxing the tightness inside her. Deni's fear eased before a wash of relief and also desire. Jace put his hand in hers, and she leaned into him, wanting to twine herself around his big body again.

Sean came to them, sword on his back glinting, and took Deni's other hand as the Shifters formed circles. "Smart idea, Deni. I commend you," he said. Then his nostrils widened, taking in her scent combined with Jace's. His gaze sharpened as it moved over Jace's mussed hair and Deni's hastily tied sarong. "Shite," he said to Jace. "You've been in Austin, what, twenty minutes? You didn't even stop for a meal first."

Deni went hot again, though she kept her head up under Sean's scrutiny and made herself meet his gaze.

"Keep it down," Jace said. "Don't embarrass the lady."

"Only if *you* can keep it down." Sean didn't burst into laughter, but his big smile showed amusement enough.

"Shut up, both of you," Deni said, certain her face must be burgundy red. "They're here."

Every law enforcement agency in this county must have answered whatever call had reported Shifters up here. Cars and SUVs surrounded the arena, floodlights glaring over the circles of Shifters, gleaming in eyes, glinting on Collars. Police in bulletproof vests swarmed out of the vehicles and into the arena, carrying guns, chains, nets, and tranq rifles. They'd come prepared to round up all of them.

The cops stopped when they found, not Shifters fighting in primitive frenzy, but Shifters and humans standing in quiet circles. The largest circle, where Deni and Jace stood, outlined the perimeter of the arena floor, with concentric circles inside it, smaller and smaller as they neared the middle of the arena. The circles of Shifters moved slowly, each one in the direction opposite of the one before it, the Shifters walking in a slow, shuffling gait. The smallest circle ringed around Dylan, Glory, and Dylan's grandson, Connor, who stood in front of a trashcan full of fire.

Shifters held hands—or had tails wrapped around hands, if they were still in animal form—and chanted a prayer to the Goddess as they moved. Each Shifter spoke quietly, but the mingling voices reverberated to the starry sky.

Deni clasped Jace's hand tightly on one side, Sean's on the other. Sean should technically be in the innermost circle with his father and nephew, but he'd stopped to make sure Deni was all right and hadn't had time to reach it.

Sean had his gaze on the inner circle and his father, but Jace looked at the ground, his shoulders hunching. The posture made him appear smaller than he was, less challenging, just another Shifter in the bunch. Deni understood why. Jace wasn't supposed to be in Texas at all. If the human police discovered he was from the Las Vegas Shiftertown, here without official permission, he'd be arrested, and things could only go downhill from there.

Shifters weren't allowed to leave the states where their Shiftertowns were located without special permits, and Jace didn't have one. Deni knew that without asking —permission was difficult to obtain and took forever. Jace had been coming and going from the Austin Shiftertown when he pleased for the last year or so, to work with Dylan and Liam on the Collars. Shifters like Jace had figured out how to go where they wanted whenever they wanted, but humans didn't need to know that. If one of the cops realized that Jace wasn't from around here ...

Deni moved her body so both she and Sean shielded Jace from the cops who stopped closest to them.

The police had halted in uncertainty, but they kept their weapons trained on the Shifters, tranq guns at the ready. The two cops in charge, a man and a woman, pushed their way through the circles of Shifters until they reached Dylan in the center.

"Tell me what the hell is going on here," the man said, his pistol trained on Dylan.

Dylan gave him a cold look. "A Shifter religious ceremony." His words came clearly, and the Shifters stopping chanting and fell silent. "What does it look like?"

"What kind of religious ceremony?" the male cop asked, not impressed. "Explain it to me."

"It's private." Dylan's voice held an edge.

"Keep it together, Dad," Sean whispered next to Deni. His gaze was on Dylan, as though he could will his father to stay calm.

"I can arrest everyone," the cop said to Dylan. "And question each and every one of you. I have the manpower and the time. Or I can arrest you by yourself, Morrissey. Your choice."

Connor spoke up, his voice shrill and sounding a few years younger than he was. "It's a memorial ceremony. For my dad."

A few of the cops moved uneasily, but most of them went more rigid.

"Who's your dad?" the male cop asked.

Dylan answered, "Kenny Morrissey. My son. He died twelve years ago. We're remembering him tonight."

"Remembering him how?"

Dylan shrugged, keeping his voice steady. "Prayers, the circle dance. We usually burn photos or other mementoes." He gestured at the flames in the trashcan next to them. "Kenny was well liked, and his brother is now the Shiftertown leader. Everyone wanted to come."

"What about fights?" the cop asked. "Bouts between humans and Shifters?"

Dylan scowled. "I don't know what shit people have been telling you, but Shifter religious ceremonies are peaceful." That was absolute truth. "No violence in any of them."

"Not what I heard," the cop said. "Cuff him," he told the female cop beside him.

Connor started forward in anguish but both Dylan and Glory stepped in his way. "It's all right, lad," Dylan said. He gave the two cops a nod. "You don't have to cuff me. I'm happy to come with you and explain everything. I bet someone told you a bunch of Shifters had gathered here, and it made your higher-ups nervous."

"Something like that," the cop said, his tone still sharp.

The woman moved forward with the cuffs. Dylan gave her a resigned look and held out his hands. "If I come with you, the others go home."

"You don't have a choice," the male cop said. "But, sure, the others can go home. In fact, they need to go, *now*. My officers will escort them out. If I like what you say downtown, then they can stay home."

Sean released Deni's hand. "I'd better go with them," he said in a low voice. "Dad can scare the shite out of people just by looking at them. I'm more diplomatic." He said it without boasting. "Ronan," he called. "Make sure Connor and Glory get home all right."

"You got it, Sean," Ronan said.

"Ride with me," Jace whispered to Deni as Sean walked away and the Shifters and humans began to disperse. The cops started herding everyone out to the parking lot, Shifters growling and rumbling in annoyance, but not arguing, their human friends walking along quietly.

"I came with Ronan and Elizabeth," Deni said nervously. She knew Jace had ridden in on a motorcycle—she'd heard it when he'd pulled up.

"I need to pretend I didn't come alone. Ronan and Elizabeth will understand."

Deni knew Jace was trying to make himself look as though he belonged in this Shiftertown. If he went off with Deni, as though part of the community, he might escape scrutiny. But that meant Deni would have to climb onto the back of a motorcycle.

"What happened to you?" another cop asked before Deni could answer Jace.

Deni stopped short, but the man wasn't talking to her. He was looking behind them, at Ronan, his tranq rifle pointed at the big man.

Ronan did look bad, his arms cut and bruised, one eye swollen. He'd skimmed on clothes while the cops were closing in, and Elizabeth now had her arm firmly around him. "I'm a bouncer," Ronan said. "At a bar. Humans like to throw punches at me." He shrugged. "I let them."

The cop gave him a look of suspicion, but he didn't pursue it. Instead he stepped in front of Jace and gave him a belligerent scowl. "What about you? You let humans take punches at you too?"

Jace's face, neck, and torso, bared by his open jacket, bore bruises from his fight with Broderick. Deni realized something she hadn't earlier—a few of the marks on Jace's neck were from her fingers, some from her teeth. She flushed.

Jace gave the cop a lazy smile without lifting his head all the way. He draped his arm around Deni and pressed a kiss to her hair. "Religious ceremonies can be boring," he said, his voice slightly slurred. "Found something better to do for a while."

The cop got a knowing look, and Deni blushed harder. Well, Jace wasn't lying. What they'd done in the darkness had been swift, hot, and glorious, not boring at all.

"Yeah, well, keep it at home," the cop said.

"Love to." Jace kept up his careless slouch, leaning on Deni, his arm around her.

The cop, fortunately, left them alone, looking around for others to harass.

"You'll have to drive," Jace said when they reached the bike. Deni thought she recognized it as belonging to Liam, who must have lent it to Jace. "I acted a little drunk so he'd leave us alone, but if he's watching, I don't want to give him an excuse to stop me for DUI." He gave her a grin and dangled the keys in front of her. "So tonight you're my designated driver."

CHAPTER THREE

D eni gazed at the keys Jace pressed into her hand, and blind panic washed through her. "I can't." She couldn't draw a breath. "Jace, I'm sorry. I can't."

"Can't?" Jace frowned down at her, his expression a mixture of compassion, curiosity, and the need to hurry. "Why? Never driven a motorcycle before?"

"I have. I own one. Or, I did. It's just ..." Deni's body was cold, fear pumping through her. "I was in a wreck on my motorcycle," she said in a rush. "A man ran me off the road last year, on purpose. I was badly hurt—took me a long time to recover. I haven't been able to ride a motorcycle since then. Plus I have ... episodes. I don't know what I'm doing for stretches of time—I've even attacked my own family. I start to go feral. Like tonight, when I fought, and when we—"

"Hey," Jace interrupted her hurried flow of words, his voice warm in the darkness. "Stop. It's all right."

"It's not all right. It's a long way from all right." Deni

drew a shuddering breath. "I haven't been able to so much as get *on* a motorcycle, not even to ride with someone else. I panic—I can't do it. Sorry, I should have told you."

"Yeah, well, we didn't get much chance to talk, did we?" Jace's eyes glinted, the teasing light in them making her both embarrassed and relieved.

She handed the keys out to him. "Thanks for understanding."

Jace didn't take them. "I mean, I get that this is hard for you, Den, but you're still going to have to drive the bike. Sorry, sweetheart, I can't risk getting stopped or arrested, or even questioned. If they find out who I am, things could get bad. Not only for me, but my father, Liam, Dylan— maybe all Shifters." He slowed his words, as though sensing Deni's fear escalate again. "You'll be all right. I'll be with you."

The keys were heavy in her hand. "Oh, right. So I won't black out and crash us, because you'll be on the seat behind me?"

"Something like that." Jace brushed his hand over her arm, his fingers blunt and warm.

Deni's fear was too raw to be easily calmed, but she was grateful to him for trying. She knew she had to get on the damned bike and take them out of there—he was right about that—but she couldn't make her feet move.

One of the cops was looking their way. The man waited a beat or two, then started for them.

Jace gave Deni a small shove toward the motorcycle. "We've got to go." Another push, moving her another step. "Only for a few miles. Once we're off their radar, we can switch."

"I can't ride in *this*." Deni gestured to herself, the fabric wrapped around her body. She had, in fact, ridden in a sarong before, but the wind would be cold and chafing. Maybe he'd take pity on her and find someone else to take him to Shiftertown.

Jace slid out of his denim jacket and draped it around her shoulders. That left his torso bare, but he didn't seem the more vulnerable for it. "You can wear this."

The jacket held his body heat and his scent. Deni closed her eyes. She looked for something peaceful inside herself, a place she used to be able to find. Jace would be with her. He'd make sure they reached Shiftertown. She willed herself to believe.

"*Now*," Jace said in her ear.

Deni jumped, but his voice galvanized her. She took a deep breath and started to swing her leg over the bike.

It got stuck halfway. Deni's heart thumped—*hurry, hurry*—but she couldn't make her leg go over the seat. She clenched her muscles, willing her body to obey, but she was shaking, her breath leaving her.

Jace swarmed onto the bike behind her, shoving her leg all the way over with his. There, she was on, with Jace wrapping his warm, bare arms around her.

The motorcycle was big—Liam, who owned it, was a big man—but Shifter women were tall. Deni could ride it.

Deni trembled all over as she started the bike, her body brushing back against the solid warmth of Jace's. The motorcycle rumbled beneath them, the deep throb of a well-tuned Harley, which let every vehicle near it know what a powerhouse it was.

Jace tightened his arms around her, pretending to have

to cling hard because he was drunk, but he turned the hold into a steadying one. Deni relaxed a little, enough to glide the bike forward, lifting her feet smoothly as they went.

The narrow road back to the highway was dark, rutted, and unnerving. The headlight sliced through blackness, the Texas night vast. Far ahead, tiny lights marked where other Shifters were driving away.

Deni started to calm even more. Her body instinctively knew how to balance the bike, how to guide the big machine, even when the road was rough. Her panic lessened, but then, out here, there were no other cars, no city streets, no humans running their vehicles into Shifters and ruining their lives.

Jace's arms around Deni, his warm body at her back, reminded her of their wild coupling, beautiful for all its brutality. Jace had a tall, strong body, one Deni would be willing to climb again. And again. Deni wished she and Jace could be truly alone, racing down the road, nothing on their minds but the wind, stars, and what they'd do together at the journey's end.

They reached the highway, the traffic sparse. Deni swung the bike to the right, heading for the lights of civilization. Austin glowed on the horizon, the city beckoning.

Deni had grown to love Austin and its quirkiness—the music, Sixth Street on a Saturday night, bars that ranged from upscale to shabby honky-tonks, the bats emerging every sunset from the Congress Avenue Bridge, the town's sense of being different from everyplace else in the world, even from the rest of Texas. Deni had found something like happiness settling here, with her brother, Ellison, and her sons, Will and Jackson. Not the greatest existence, living in Shiftertown, but at least they were together.

And then the bastard human, who'd been involved in some nasty business regarding Shifters that Ellison and Deni had helped clear up, had deliberately run down Deni on her motorcycle, robbing her of control and any sense of tranquility. Tonight, coupling with Jace and now having him hold on to her was the closest she'd come to finding peace again.

Deni turned onto the 183 and headed north. She was sure Jace would tell her to pull over any minute so he could take over the driving, but he didn't. Jace kept his arms around her, his body leaning with hers as she made the turn and joined traffic.

Deni started to shake again as traffic thickened, cars and trucks surging around them to head for Austin from points east of San Antonio. Jace's warm hands moved on Deni's belly, as though he knew she needed his reassuring touch. Deni felt a little better, but when they reached Lockhart, she pulled off to a gas station.

"You can take over now," she said, sliding off the helmet.

Jace didn't dismount. "You're doing fine. Keep going."

"Jace, come on. I'm scared. The wreck really messed me up. The guy who did it was trying to grab me—he was kidnapping Shifters."

Jace's eyes narrowed. "I heard about him. He didn't get you though, right?"

"Only because there were too many other people around. He nearly killed me."

"But he's dead now." Jace spoke with conviction. Dylan must have told him some of that story.

"Yes." Deni swallowed, her mouth dry. She wondered if Dylan had told Jace exactly how the man had died, and Deni's part in it. "My mind knows that I'm safe, but my instincts don't. The wolf inside me hasn't fully processed it yet, I guess."

Jace kept frowning. "I see that. But I'm right here with you. Show yourself you can do it. Don't let him win."

Deni wanted to—she truly did. Her brother had given her similar advice: *Don't let the asshole take everything away from you.*

Wise words, but still, it was hard. "What if I black out?"

Jace shot her a grin. "I'll wake you up."

"Jace, I *can't.*"

"You're wrong. You can."

Deni grasped the handlebars. She used to love to ride, she and Ellison going all out on the back roads, side by side, racing. She missed it.

She gave Jace a challenging look. "What if I get off right here and refuse to ride?"

Jace shrugged. "Then I take the bike back to Liam and send you a cab. Or you can shift to wolf and go cross-country."

"Oh, thanks."

The grin returned. "Or, you can drive."

He was a shithead. A sexy one. Damn it.

Everything in Deni wanted to do this. Waiting at this gas station for a cab certainly didn't appeal to her, especially not with the few good old boys starting to eye them.

Humans and Shifters weren't supposed to tangle, but out in farm and ranch country, in the middle of the night, rules didn't always stop anyone.

Deni slapped the helmet back on her head. She revved the bike and pulled out of the gas station, opening up the engine once she got out of town to make it throb.

Wind rushed past her, the bike rumbled under her, and Jace, hard-bodied and hot, hung on to her. Deni still felt the ache of their rough lovemaking, and knew she carried his seed inside her. What would happen if that seed took root? The thought of having another cub frightened her almost as much as riding did, but it elated her at the same time.

Deni navigated them onto the 130 then off when the 183 split from it again, and kept on straight north for Austin. She was sweating by the time they hit Austin proper, Jace's jacket cutting the bracing wind. The increasing traffic made her panic rise once more, but Jace was there, caressing her, his touch calming.

Excitement hit Deni when she rolled into the mostly deserted streets around Shiftertown and pulled the motorcycle up behind the bar Liam managed. She swung off the bike after Jace dismounted, and yanked off her helmet.

"I did it. Goddess, Jace—I did it!"

"Yeah, you did." Jace swept his arms around her and pulled her against him. "You were great. And you didn't even pass out."

Deni was too buoyed to respond to the remark. She gave him a hard kiss on the mouth, loving the taste of him. Her excitement increased, her need for him not slaked.

Jace didn't discourage her. His kiss turned hard, his hands on her back strong.

Deni made herself ease away from him, though he remained holding her a moment, his eyes dark green in the moonlight. Shaking a little, Deni stepped back, slid his jacket off, and handed it back to him, though it was a shame to watch him cover himself.

Jace shrugged the jacket on then took a backpack from one of the saddlebags and slung it over his shoulder. He put his arm around Deni. "Come in and have a beer with me?"

This was Deni's chance to tell him she needed to go home, to wait for her sons to get in from work, her brother and his mate to return from their date. To go back to watching everyone else live, while she sat in the corner and tried to stay sane.

To hell with that. Deni squared her shoulders, slid her hand through Jace's offered arm, and walked in with him through the back door.

They emerged into the loud bar, half full of Shifters. A tall Shifter covered in tatts spied them and stepped in front of Jace.

"Liam wants to see you," he said with his characteristic brevity, then turned around and walked away.

"That's Spike," Deni said. "Man of few words."

"I've met him." Jace took Deni's hand and led her through the crowd, making his way to the black-haired Irishman leaning on the bar. He wasn't tending it—Shifters weren't allowed to serve alcohol. A human barman did that.

Liam Morrissey turned as they approached, as though

sensing them come, which he probably had. He wouldn't have been able to hear them over the jukebox, or smell them over the odors of smoke, alcohol, sweaty humans, and Shifters who'd also just returned from the fight club. But Liam had the uncanny knack of knowing where everyone was at all times. Liam was tall, like his brother, Sean, and had the same intense blue eyes. Those eyes took in Jace, then Deni, then Liam leaned forward and pulled Jace into a Shifter welcoming embrace.

Jace dropped his backpack on a barstool and let Liam enfold him. Because the two had met before and liked each other, the hug was more cordial and less wary than many alpha male exchanges. No veiled hint that each would rip out the other's throat if they had half a chance. Just friendship and camaraderie, arms tightening on each other's backs.

Liam released Jace, turned to Deni, and pulled her into his arms as well. This hug was more reassuring, the Shiftertown leader trying to calm one of his own. "Well done," Liam said quietly into her ear, and Deni warmed with pleasure.

Liam released Deni and found Jace right next to him. *Right* next to him, as in slap up against him. Jace's eyes had tightened, and he pinned Liam with a warning stare.

Liam reached past Jace for a half-filled bottle of beer he'd left on the bar and held it without drinking. "Spike and Ronan told me what happened out there with the cops." He gave Deni a grin. "I see you two already celebrated."

As she had under Sean's scrutiny, Deni flushed, but

Jace looked unworried. "Have you heard anything from Dylan?" Jace asked him.

Liam lost his smile. "They took Dad downtown. My mate is with him, and so is Sean. They told me not to come." He nodded, as though he agreed. "Kim knows what she's doing."

Liam's mate was a defense lawyer who now specialized in defending Shifters. Liam was right that she was plenty competent, and Dylan and Sean were good at keeping human attention away from Shifters. Deni saw the tightness in Liam, however, sensed his need to race to the police station and use any means necessary to extract his father.

"Did the police talk to you?" Jace asked him.

"Aye, they did. Came rushing in here, demanding to know about this fight club they'd heard about. Of course, I knew nothing, did I?" Liam, as leader, had decided to look the other way about the fight club, which went against Shifter laws as well as human. Though the fight clubs had rules, they were dangerous, but Liam had acknowledged long ago that he couldn't prevent them. "A detective and half a dozen uniforms came in here the same time the arena was being raided, or I would have warned my dad and Sean." Deni saw the outrage in his eyes that he'd been blindsided.

"Well, they found it somehow," Jace said. "You have a leak. Just to reassure you—it isn't me."

"Didn't think it was, lad."

If Liam *had* thought Jace was the one who'd betrayed the whereabouts of the fight club, Jace wouldn't be standing here speaking calmly to Liam. He'd have been stopped at the door, and Liam would now be disemboweling him in the parking lot.

"Do we lie low?" Jace asked.

Liam answered with one quick shake of his head but no words. Not all Shifters were privy to the work Liam and his family were doing on the Collars. Need to know only. Most Shifters were trustworthy, but as tonight had proved, leaks happened.

Liam looked at Deni again and started to smile. "A memorial service. Good thinking, lass." He chuckled.

"It was the first logical thing I could think of," Deni said. "I'm sorry I used your family's grief as a distraction."

Liam shook his head, his eyes bright with mirth. "Kenny would have laughed his balls off. He always loved a good joke, did Kenny."

Liam was grinning, but Deni saw the moisture in his eyes, his sorrow for his dead brother never far away.

"Then we'll meet as appointed," Jace broke in. "Unless you wave me off."

"Aye, get some rest." Liam's amusement returned as he turned to Deni again. "*Rest*, mind. Looks like you need it." He gave her a quiet nod. "Like I said, well done, lass."

"Leader's pet," Jace whispered in Deni's ear as he guided her through the crowded bar, his hand on the small of her back. His laugh did warm things to her. "Let's get you home."

———

WALKING DENI HOME WAS DELAYED WHEN BRODERICK came into the bar, followed by Shifters looking enough like him to be his brothers. Jace felt Deni's rage and worry increase, her body vibrating under his hand.

"We don't like outsiders," one of Broderick's brothers said, stepping in front of Jace. "Don't like them coming in and taking our women."

Deni was around Jace before he saw her move. "Suck on it," Deni said. "I thought I was too crazy for you all, anyway."

Broderick showed his teeth in a smile. "She's got good reflexes, for a nutcase."

Jace pulled Deni back behind him and moved to Broderick, the clear leader of this bunch. "Keep your shit to yourself and your brothers quiet," he said, "or I'll wipe the floor with your ass. Again."

Broderick glanced around Jace to Deni, and his eyes widened as he realized what other Shifters had been all night—that Jace and Deni had gotten to know each other in the dark out at the fight club. Broderick lifted his hands. "Hey, if you're that frenzied by her, you take her. You'll be doing us all a favor. Hope you can keep her under control."

Jace had Broderick by the throat before Broderick could blink. Jace surprised even himself with the move, and his speed. "What did I just tell you?"

Jace was aware of Shifters turning, watching, stilling. The music pumped on, a loud country song, but the Shifters stopped dancing, talking, and drinking to watch.

Broderick's brother was right about one thing—Jace was an outsider. He was a dominant and sanctioned by Dylan and Liam, but that wouldn't matter if the entire Shifter community didn't want him. A pack, en masse, could kill an alpha and not care.

He felt Deni behind him—close behind him—pressed against his back, but she wasn't trying to soothe him out of his rage or stop him. Jace sensed her excitement, her uncontrolled need to fight. If he followed up his threat on Broderick, Deni would be right beside him, battling it out with him. The thought made him warm, gave him strength.

Liam was still at the bar, watching. Doing nothing. He wanted to see how Jace would handle this.

Letting Broderick go would decrease Jace's standing in this Shiftertown. Not letting him go might get him killed.

A very large hand landed on Jace's shoulder, another on Broderick's. Jace got a whiff of an annoyed Kodiak bear Shifter who hadn't showered since his arena fight.

"Take it out of the bar, boys," Ronan said. "Better idea —Broderick, you stay here and get rat-faced drunk like you do every night, and you..." He gave Jace the slightest shake. "You go and sleep it off. You're supposed to be holing up at Dylan's house, but he's off trying to stay out of jail. Take Deni home, and crash on Ellison's couch."

Ronan, as bouncer, was breaking the impasse. Smart. Ronan's intervention let Jace save face, and Broderick didn't get his ass handed to him. Jace had no doubt that Liam had signaled Ronan somehow, but Liam still watched as though only mildly interested.

Jace eased the pressure of his fingers around Broderick's throat. Broderick's Collar sparked once, jumping electricity into Jace's hand, but Jace didn't jerk away. He opened his fingers slowly and lowered his arm. Broderick remained where he was, not stepping back or rubbing his neck, which was imprinted with Jace's finger marks.

Jace deliberately turned away from him. "Good idea,"

Jace said to Ronan. "By the way, you fought a good fight out there."

Ronan gave him a brief nod of thanks, but he moved himself solidly between Jace and Broderick. If they decided to go for each other again, they'd have to do it around the wall of Ronan. Jace might outrank Ronan in dominance, but there was no disputing that Ronan was huge.

Jace took a step back, showing he wouldn't push it, and held his hand out to Deni.

He sensed Deni's relief as she took his hand, but also her disappointment that another fight with Broderick wouldn't ensue. She said nothing to Jace, only gave Broderick a final glare, and then Jace led Deni to the door and out into the night.

Deni started walking swiftly once they left the bar, moving faster and faster, until she was nearly dragging Jace across the empty lot and toward the streets of Shiftertown. In the middle of the dusty, weed-choked field, Jace pulled her to a halt.

"Hold up," he said. "Tell me something—what the hell was that?"

Deni's gray eyes gleamed in the darkness. "What the hell was what?"

"You." Jace pointed his finger at her face. "Egging me on in there. Not *Be careful, Jace, you don't want to get yourself into trouble.* More like, *Go on, Jace. Kick his ass!* You wanted to see me get taken down by that whole bar, did you?"

"No." Deni clenched her hands, as though resisting the urge to nibble the end of his finger. "Broderick just pisses me off. And you wouldn't have been taken down by the whole bar. I saw you fight—they'd have backed off."

"Were you this bloodthirsty before your accident?"

Deni hesitated, her chest rising with her breath. "I don't know."

Jace put his hands on her arms, which were cold. The night was cooling, and her flesh, bared by the sarong, rose in goose bumps. "You said fighting makes you want to fight," he said. "But we weren't fighting in there. Not yet."

"But you wanted to." Deni rested her fingers on Jace's forearms. "I sensed that loud and clear. You were ready to rip out Broderick's throat. I can take his crap, but you couldn't. Are *you* always this bloodthirsty?"

Not until today. He made himself grin. "Everyone at home thinks I'm reasonable and a peacemaker." *Good old Jace. He'll calm everyone down.*

"Yeah? Not sure I'd want to meet your family, then."

"You would. You'd like my dad, and his mate." He rubbed her arms. "Too cold out here. Let's get you home."

Deni shivered, as though realizing how lightly dressed she was. "Fine. Though I'm not sure about you sleeping on the couch. Liam might have room at his house. Or Spike might."

She started to turn away. Jace thought about finding space in a dark house that didn't contain her, and something kicked him in the gut.

Jace dragged her back to him. Deni landed against his chest, her gray eyes going wide. He felt her heart beating rapidly as he scooped her to him, slid his hand to the back of her neck, and pulled her up for a hard kiss.

CHAPTER FOUR

Their mouths met in a frenzy. Deni clung to Jace, her breath hot on his lips, her kisses wild, hungry.

Jace wrapped his arms around her. This woman, this delicious female, was awakening something he'd never felt before—need, primal and intense, which all Shifters possessed, but which Jace had only experienced dimly before this. Even the hormonal craziness of his Transition to adulthood hadn't spiked the intense desire through him that kissing Deni did.

As her strong hands pulled him down to her, Jace realized she needed him in return. Needed *him*, Jace the man, not Jace the Shifter leader's son—she hadn't known who he was when they'd met. Nothing in her behavior, her scent, her voice had told him she cared where he was in the food chain.

She rose on tiptoes, running fingers through his short hair, kissing him as though she couldn't get enough. Jace felt his frenzy reply—*need, mate, don't let go.*

Deni pushed away from him with a suddenness that robbed him of breath. Cold air filled in where she'd been, and Jace felt suddenly empty.

Deni was staring up at him, her chest rising with her agitation. "Sorry. I can't control—"

Jace's returning breath hurt him. "It's not control I'm looking for."

"I am."

Because of her accident, she meant, her fear it was making her go feral. "I get that." Jace clasped her elbows. "But that's over, Deni. You survived. I won't let you lose it when you're with me. I promise."

She shuddered. "I just wish—"

"Wish what?" Jace drew her closer again, running his hands up her arms to cup her shoulders. "Tell me what you want."

"To be normal again. A year ago, I would have snatched up someone like you, taken you somewhere private, and not come out until we were done enjoying ourselves."

Jace grinned down at her. "Me too. With you, I mean."

"But now." Deni shuddered but she didn't pull away. "I'm afraid to let myself go."

"Yeah," Jace said, his voice quieter. "Me too." That's why they'd sent Jace to Austin to liaise and test the Collar control problem. Jace was trustworthy, dependable. Could keep a secret. Could take pain and not go crazy from it. He didn't need anyone to hold his hand, never had.

He liked to stay in control, be strong. But tonight ...

"Come on," Deni said. She laced her hand through his, tugging him along with her. "Best I get home."

Jace's heart still thrummed from the kiss, Deni's taste, her scent, the warmth of her body imprinted on his. The feral being deep inside him growled in frustration, wanting out.

Keep it together. He was supposed to be helping Deni stay calm. But as Jace walked behind her, watching her hips sway while her hand was hot in his, he wondered which of them would prove to be the stronger.

WILL AND JACKSON, DENI'S SONS, WERE HOME. DENI'S heart lightened when she saw their pickup in the driveway and the lights glowing in the house. Home. Safety.

Jace's scent like wild sage wrapped around her as she led him up onto the porch. Her idea that he could go sleep at Liam's or Spike's didn't seem as good now. Deni didn't like the thought of him saying good-bye and walking away.

"Sweet ride," Jace said, gesturing at the motorcycle parked next to the pickup. "Yours?"

Deni nodded, her heart squeezing. "Ellison bought it for me after mine was totaled." She glanced at it and turned resolutely away.

"And you haven't ridden it," Jace said. "Shame."

"Isn't it?" Deni jerked open the door to the house. She was *not* going to let Jace talk her into getting on the motor-cycle tonight. She'd done well riding Liam's bike home, but she still shook from it. Too much too soon.

Jace followed her inside without further word. Deni entered her haven, filled with the scents of her sons, her brother, and his mate. Soon her brother and mate would have their first cub, and more laughter would fill the house.

"Mom."

Will, her youngest, already twenty-four, came to Deni as she entered the kitchen and wrapped his arms around her. She hugged him back, her beloved son. After a long time, Will lifted his head, looked her up and down, and asked, "What the hell happened to you?"

"Fight," Deni said. "But I'm okay. I rode, Will. Liam's bike—all the way from the fight club."

Will's eyes widened, but Jackson, two years older than Will, said, "And you were at the fight club, why?" He came forward, greeting Deni by giving her a hug from the side. Will hadn't moved.

Neither son acknowledged Jace standing quietly near the door. Will and Jackson were still technically cubs, though they were in their twenties—adults in human terms. They hadn't gone through their Transitions yet. They were clinging to Deni as instinctively as they had when they'd been tiny, waiting for her to either tell them the strange Shifter was a friend, or for them to join together to attack him.

Deni also knew they scented Jace on her, and her on him, and known what they'd done. Before the accident, they'd have started teasing her. Now they waited, uncertain.

"This is Jace Warden," she said. "He's staying with us tonight."

"Oh yeah?" Jackson finally eyed Jace, though he didn't go so far as to pin him with a defiant stare. "Why's that?"

"Dylan invited him out here," Deni said. "But Dylan's been arrested."

As she'd guessed, the announcement made the boys put aside their nervousness and barrage her with questions, starting with *What? Are you serious?*

Jace helped Deni fill them in on the story. Once Will and Jackson were more relaxed with Jace, Deni went to her room, washed up, changed her clothes, then returned to the kitchen and started putting together sandwiches. Big ones. She was *hungry.*

The boys and Jace devoured everything she set down on the table. Deni watched her sons relax even more as Jace talked. He really did have the knack of putting everyone at ease.

The sight of him hulking at the table, shoveling down roast beef, ham, and turkey on three different kinds of bread while Will and Jackson hung on his words made Deni's heart ache again. This is what she should have had with her mate and cubs—a family, laughing, talking, eating, sharing. Deni's mate had died of illness long ago, robbing Deni of the life she'd wanted. Being shoveled into a Shiftertown had been even more bewildering. But they'd made it, she, Ellison, Jackson, and Will.

Here they were, and now Jace seemed to complete the picture.

"Seriously, Mom," Will said, his mouth full. "Why did you go to the fight club? You know what happens ..."

Deni reached across the table for the butter and slapped some onto her slab of bread. "Because I was tired of sitting at home huddled up in a shawl. Ronan and Elizabeth offered to give me a lift to the fight club, and I took them up on it. I thought it would do me good to get out and have fun."

"You could have gone to the bar," Jackson said, frowning. "Safer."

"Not really. Too many human groupies looking for a Shifter to grope. Plus, all my friends were at the fights tonight. I wanted to go." Deni gave Jackson a motherly glare, and he shrugged.

"Speaking of groping ..." Jackson trailed off, deliberately not looking at Jace or Deni. Will snorted as he took another bite.

"None of your business," Deni said.

Jace said nothing at all, only looked amused. He betrayed no shame, no regret for their quick encounter in the darkness.

The boys got their snickering in, but Deni could tell they were relieved. Had they thought their mom was washed-up? Out of life because she sometimes went out of her mind? That maybe no other Shifter would want her?

Jace remained silent, letting them laugh. At one point, he caught Deni's gaze and winked, and Deni's blood started to simmer. It really was dangerous to have him here.

Jackson and Will retreated to their room after the meal to watch videos and sleep. Jace came to Deni where she looked out the window across the street, wondering if Dylan would return tonight, and wrapped his arms around her from behind.

"They love you," he said.

Deni leaned back into his warmth. "They're my cubs."

"It's good to see." Jace let out his breath, heat tickling her ear. "I never knew my mother. She died bringing me in."

Deni heard the sorrow in his words. She pressed her hand over his. "I'm so sorry."

"It's always made me a little touchy, you know?" Jace held her tighter. "Afraid to get too close to anyone. It can happen so fast, losing someone."

So true. "You have your dad," she said. "And the rest of your family." Though she knew no one could ever take the place of a lost loved one.

"I do. And my dad has done some shit that's scared me to death, trust me." Jace gave a little chuckle. "But it's made me careful."

Careful. Deni had learned to be that as well.

His closeness made her nervous, and not because she didn't like it. Deni broke his hold and turned around. "Hope the couch is comfortable. Linens are in the closet in the hall."

His gaze sought hers. "I'm sure it will be." He touched her throat above her Collar, fingertips caressing. His jade green eyes darkened, but he didn't speak. Whatever his thoughts were, he kept them to himself.

"Good night, then." Deni rose on her tiptoes and gently kissed his lips.

Jace slid one arm around her, turning the kiss into something deeper. His mouth was a point of heat in the darkness, their lips meeting in silence.

Jace eased away, taking his hands from Deni and

balling them into fists, as though stopping himself from reaching for her again. "Good night," he said.

Deni swallowed, but didn't move. "Good night."

Jace took a step back. "You'd better go."

Good thinking. If Deni stayed, she'd grab him, and they'd go down right here in the living room. Another chance for them both to lose control.

"Sure," she said. "If you need anything . . ."

Jace held up one hand, fingers stiff. "Don't say that. Too dangerous. Good night," he repeated, firmly.

Deni nodded and made herself turn around, walk down the small hallway, and enter her bedroom. She looked back before she closed the door, seeing Jace standing in the living room, rigid, large, solid.

Shutting the door on him was one of the hardest things she'd ever done.

———

In the middle of the night, Collar payback hit Jace.

He opened his eyes in the dark, sweat rolling down his face, pain smacking him in the gut. He stifled his groans—no use waking up the rest of the house.

Payback happened when a Shifter prevented his Collar from going off while he was fighting. Helped a lot during the fight, but afterward there was always a backlash. The systems relaxed, the Shifter's adrenaline dissipated, and the suppressed pain woke up and said hello.

Jace's nerves were on fire. The pain started at his throat and poured from there into his body. He doubled up, still on the couch, rolling onto his side and silently fighting the agony.

Smooth, cool hands touched his skin. Jace had stripped down to his jeans to sleep but hadn't put on anything else —he'd found enough blankets in the linen cupboard to keep his bare torso comfortably warm.

Deni's touch cut through his pain. She knelt on the floor next to him, the fabric of her long T-shirt brushing his body. She wore a bracelet on her right wrist, a thin gold chain with a small charm that soothed when it touched him. She hadn't been wearing it earlier tonight, but maybe she hadn't wanted to risk it getting lost at the fight club.

Jace took a deep breath, trying to still his racing heartbeat. Deni drew her hands up his chest and across his shoulders. A few hours ago, Jace would have found the touch sexual, invigorating. Same hands, same woman, but now she calmed.

He laid his head on the arm of the sofa, forcing his body to open up from its cramped position. Deni moved her hands down his chest and to his abdomen, her touch firm but caressing.

Jace drew in another breath. Deni left swaths of relief as she pulled her hands across him, paths free from pain.

She leaned down and kissed his chest. Jace wound an arm around her and pulled her closer. It felt so natural to hold her to him like this. Maybe he'd known this woman in another life, perhaps they'd had a love for the ages there. Shifters didn't believe in reincarnation, but Jace's fogged brain liked the idea.

Deni kept kissing his body, kept stroking with her hands. Her lips were soft points on his hot skin, her hands so beautifully skilled. If Jace weren't in so much pain he'd be aroused. He'd love to pull her up to straddle him, to hold her while she found pleasure in him.

He let out a whispered groan. Deni kissed his lips, stifling the small sound.

Jace held her, moving his lips to kiss her back. Wonderful, sweet woman. Her touch unclenched the tightness in him, feathering comfort through his body.

She'd risen from her bed, somehow knowing he was in pain, and had come out here, even after the wary *good night* they'd shared. Jace had made sure he'd been as quiet as possible, but she must have heard him or sensed his pain.

Jace kissed her lips again, stroking her hair. If they had time and freedom, they'd find so much together. He was Feline, she Lupine, he from the Vegas Shiftertown, she from the Austin. Distance, family, and laws kept them apart, but at this moment—who cared?

Deni raised her head. She kissed the tip of Jace's nose and brushed her hands down his chest once more, the gold chain whispering.

"Better?" she asked.

"Much."

"Good." She unfolded to her feet, the hem of her long T-shirt brushing her knees. She leaned down, bathing Jace in her scent, and kissed his lips once more. Then her touch and kiss were gone, Deni moving down the hall to her bedroom.

Jace lay back, the vestiges of his pain fading. "Good night," he whispered, and fell into a deep, untroubled sleep.

JACE WALKED OUT OF THE HOUSE THE NEXT MORNING with Ellison Rowe, Deni's brother. He walked out, even though Deni wasn't up yet, because Ellison escorted him out.

Jace had been sleeping hard after Deni had gone to bed the second time, when he'd been jerked out of slumber by a big Shifter sitting down on him.

Both men had come off the couch with a yell of rage, then they'd faced each other across the living room rug. Ellison's pale hair had gleamed in the moonlight, his big fists clenched, his eyes wolf white. Jace stood barefoot in jeans in another Shifter's house, and for that, this pack leader had a right to tear him up.

Ellison's mate, a small human woman named Maria, had stepped between them and calmly asked Jace what he was doing here. Jace had met her before—the woman had been rescued from a feral Shifter in Mexico and brought here, and Ellison had fallen on his ass in love with her.

Once Jace explained about his visit, Dylan, and the fight club, Ellison had backed off a little. Ellison had heard about Dylan's arrest and conceded that Jace could stay. But the look on his face when he scented Deni on Jace was pure fury.

Deni hadn't woken up during the altercation, but then, they'd conducted most of it after their initial shout in silence, with only a little growling. Jace decided to take a shower, tired of people sniffing him, and by the time he'd come out, the sun was up. Ellison pointedly walked Jace out of the house and started along the street with him.

"My sister," Ellison said, "is going through some shit."

"She told me some of it." Jace hoisted his backpack on his shoulder, reflecting that he'd probably need to find someplace else to stay tonight.

"She's scared and still healing. She doesn't need to be confused."

The pissed-off feral in Jace started rising again. Why did everyone assume he was ready to take advantage of Deni? They all needed to leave her alone, give her some space.

"I'm not here to confuse her." Jace stopped, forcing Ellison to face him. Ellison had his cowboy hat and boots on—he liked to play the big, bad Texan. "Deni's a good woman."

"I know. I've lived with her all my life." Ellison's gray eyes held worry behind his anger. "Keep it cool. Don't let her ..."

He trailed off, as though unable to find the words to describe his gut-wrenching fears.

Jace dared to close the space between them, dared even more to put his hand on Ellison's shoulder. "I'd never hurt her," he said. "I can see she's special."

Ellison held Jace's gaze but softened it. "She is."

Jace squeezed his shoulder. "Then we're good."

Ellison gave him another look, then put his hand on Jace's shoulder in return. His squeeze was a little harder than necessary, but he was conceding. Two Shifters agreeing not to fight. At least, not right now.

Ellison walked away from Jace after that, and Jace continued on a few blocks to a house that was set back behind another. Behind *that,* completely hidden from the street, was a brick garage that looked like nothing more than a normal garage. Jace opened the door and walked in, to be greeted by Liam Morrissey and his brother Sean.

"Excellent," Liam said. "Dad sends his regrets ... obviously. We'll get started."

CHAPTER FIVE

"They still have Dylan?" Jace asked.

The garage he stood in had been converted to a workshop. Two long tables ran the length of the room, flanked by a few stools. Bolted to the benches were a scroll saw, a drill press, and what looked like a router in a stand. At the end of one bench was a jeweler's vise that rotated on a huge ball bearing so the worker could look at a piece from every angle.

The benches also held tools—every style of pliers and vise grips, wire snips, knives, gauges, squares, rulers, and other measuring devices. Boxes holding silver bits and jump links were arranged on the benches, and a soldering iron lay next to a can of flux.

A few half-built pieces of furniture and some trays of jewelry had been set up in the corners of the room, but Jace knew those were for verisimilitude should humans find this workshop. The true projects lay in the boxes of silver pieces. Liam and his family were making fake

Collars and also researching how to remove real Collars from Shifters without making said Shifters insane.

Sean nodded to Jace's question. "Dad's still in jail. They wanted to keep him overnight. Kim's working on it."

"She's good, is my mate," Liam said. "She'll make them see reason, or at least shove legalese at them until they choke."

Sean and Liam, in spite of their hopeful words, were worried, Jace saw. Both men had deep shadows under their eyes and moved a bit stiffly. They'd probably been up all night.

"Sure you want to be experimenting on my neck when you've had no sleep?" he asked, only half joking.

"Don't worry, lad. We won't do much today."

Sean unbuckled the Sword of the Guardian from his back, slid the blade out of its leather sheath, and laid the sword on the table. Runes that looked ancient and powerful were traced all over the sword, blade and hilt alike.

Jace had seen the sword belonging to the Guardian in his own Shiftertown, but this one, he knew, was the original. The first, made by Shifter sword maker Niall O'Connell and woven with spells by the Fae woman Alanna, had been passed down through the generations to Sean—the men of the Morrissey family were O'Connell's heirs.

Shifters didn't much go in for magic, but Jace knew the tingle of it when he felt it. There was magic in the sword, and its vibration permeated the air of the room.

"Collars," Liam said, seating himself on one of the stools. "Fae magic and human technology woven together. Cracking that code is the toughest thing."

"How's it going?" Jace asked. "Any progress?"

"Some," Liam continued while Sean sat down, laid a few pieces of silver together on the jeweler's anvil, and clicked on the light of the magnifier above it.

"We can get to the Collar's chip." Liam tapped the round black-and-silver piece that was a Celtic cross resting on his throat. "It's in there, wired up and ready to go. The magic part is in the silver that weaves through the Collar— *most* of the magic is in there, that is. What we haven't figured out is how the magic and technology tie together. That's important, because what fuses them is also, we think, what fuses the Collar to the Shifter's neck. It bites into our nervous system and stays there. That's why, when the first experimenters simply ripped Collars from necks, the Shifter's adrenaline system kicked into high gear, sending that Shifter feral. It was as though years of instincts being suppressed by the Collars suddenly sprang out, with twenty years of rage fueling them."

Jace had heard about the experiments of a few years ago, done by an idiot who hadn't cared that the Shifters went crazy when the Collars came off. He'd only wanted the Shifters free of Collars and under his thumb. Liam had been caught up in the battle to stop it. Liam, his father, and Sean had taken over the experimenting and were being much more careful about it.

Liam continued, "We have to figure out what it is that makes the Collars work as one piece. What that third element is, so to speak. Magic, technology, and something that slides in between."

"And I'm the guinea pig?" Jace asked.

"Only if you want to be, lad. We won't force you."

But this was why Jace had come. He'd learned, slowly over the last year, how to control his Collar. He'd been teaching his father and others in his Shiftertown how to do it, and preparing himself for Collar removal. The Morrisseys had learned to make fake Collars that would fool humans, but only two Shifters thus far wore them—Andrea, Sean's mate, and Tiger, a Shifter who'd been created by humans. Tiger had never worn a Collar before he came to Shiftertown, and when they'd tried to put one on, he'd gone even crazier than he already was. Liam had decided a fake Collar for Tiger was the best solution.

Andrea had worn a real Collar most of her life, but strangely, it had never worked on her. Andrea was half Fae. Sean's theory was that her Fae-ness somehow counteracted the magic inside the Collar. Or else her healing magic did—Andrea was a healer. Andrea's Collar had come off easily, in any case.

The Morrisseys were trying to apply what they'd learned from Andrea to other Shifters, but they still hadn't figured out the details. It was tough to find Shifters stable enough, trustworthy enough, and willing enough to let themselves be lab rats for the Collar experiments. Hence, Jace's trips to Austin.

Jace opened his arms and shrugged. "What do you want me to do?"

Sean picked up a soldering iron. "Be best if you held still."

Jace looked at the pencil-thin device, which hummed a little as Sean turned it on. The tip would be turning brutally hot.

"Seriously?" Jace asked him.

Sean attempted to keep a worried look off his face as he approached, which didn't make Jace feel any better. "We're trying to both find a safe way to remove the Collars and discover their secret at the same time," Sean said. "I volunteered myself, but Dad and Liam won't let me."

"Because you're the Guardian," Jace said as sweat broke out on his face. "If this kills you, ripples will be felt throughout Shiftertown—the Shifter world, even. Kill me, and the ripples will be smaller."

"No killing," Sean said quickly. "We'll stop short of killing."

"Whew." Jace's heart beat faster, but he kept his voice light. "Thank the Goddess for small favors."

"I'd love to tell you this won't hurt," Sean said. He raised the soldering iron.

Liam closed in on Jace's other side. "You going to be all right, lad? No ripping into us, I mean?"

A bead of sweat trickled down Jace's back, and he curled his hands to fists. "Let's find out."

"Dad should be here," Liam said. "But he told us not to wait."

"How did he tell you?" Jace kept his eyes on the hot tip of the iron. "He's in jail."

"He's good at getting messages to us," Sean said. "He wants us to start. He must know something."

"Possibly," Jace said. He clenched his jaw, fists tightening.

Something cold touched the side of Jace's neck. A knife—a very small, delicate one, wielded by Liam. Sean held the iron competently between steady fingers and brought it close to Jace's throat.

"The heat loosens the metal without tearing you," Liam said. His knife nicked Jace's skin, just barely.

"You know this, how?" Jace asked. Neither Sean nor Liam answered. Jace didn't want to move his throat by swallowing, but he couldn't help but lick his dry lips. "Ah, so you *don't* know."

"We've done a lot of thinking on this," Liam said. "Someone's got to be the first."

"Sean said you took Andrea's off with a knife alone."

"True, but Andrea's wasn't fused to her nervous system. Trust me, we'll do this slowly. Only a link or two today. More tomorrow if it works."

"*If* it works," Jace repeated. "Your skills at reassurance are terrific, Liam. What a hell of a Shiftertown leader you must make."

"Stop talking," Liam said. "Stay very, very still."

Jace was doing this for the good of all Shifters, he reminded himself. Shifters for years to come would benefit from Jace's sacrifice.

It was that word—*sacrifice*—that Jace was having trouble with at the moment.

The knife blade cut. At the same time, Sean darted in with the iron. Searing heat radiated across Jace's neck and down his spine. He felt a wildcat snarl begin deep inside but he tamped it down as hard as he could. If he shifted now, who the hell knew what would happen to him?

Liam and Sean backed off as swiftly as they'd gone in. Jace opened his eyes and shook his head, the pain easing. He blinked, realizing he viewed the other two through cat's eyes. He relaxed his hands and found he'd gouged his own palms with leopard claws.

He drew a ragged breath, willing all of himself to resume human form. "Is that it?"

Liam shook his head. "Started it. A little bit more, and we'll have a link or two off. Then drinks are on me."

"It's eight in the morning."

"I'm thinking you won't care what time it is when we're done, lad. Plus, you had one hell of a night last night. So did we. Beer is a good thing."

Jace drew in a deep breath through his nose. "All right," he said. He released the breath. "I'm ready."

Sean jammed the iron onto Liam's knife blade, and the searing knife slid under Jace's skin. "Oh, son of a f—" Jace's words became a wildcat snarl. He slammed his eyes shut, not wanting to see the world rock if he shifted.

The process took longer this time. Liam's breath brushed Jace's neck as he leaned close, his lion's scent different enough from the Feline scents Jace had grown up with to make his leopard a little crazy.

After an agonizing stretch of time, Liam stepped back, Sean took away the iron, and the pain, mercifully, let up. Jace opened his eyes again, taking deep breaths until his killing instincts calmed down.

His clothes were drenched with sweat, his body shaking. Jace wiped his face with the back of his hand and moved his fingers toward his neck.

"Careful," Liam said. "That's going to be a little tender."

A little? Jace barely brushed himself and jerked his hand away at the raw pain. "Is it off?"

"A link and a half," Liam said. "Good for today."

"A link and a half?" Jace spun to a grimy mirror over a

sink. Sure enough, a link had loosened on the right side of his neck. Beneath it was an angry red mark. "We can't let anyone see this."

"No," Liam agreed, while Sean turned off the iron. "I suggest a scarf or a jacket."

Jacket. Jace had brought a hoodie for cooler nights, and Liam had pulled the link where such a thing could hide the traces.

Jace rummaged in his backpack. The cloth of the jacket, when it settled against his neck, stung, but the small hurt was nothing to what had gone through him before.

"What now?" Jace asked.

"Beer," Sean said, sliding his sword back into its scabbard. "Lots of it. And trying to spring my dad from jail."

———

Deni kept busy in her yard after Will and Jackson left for work. Maria had gone off to school, and Ellison was back, snoring in his bedroom, sleeping off his night, leaving Deni relatively alone. She didn't want to sit in the house waiting to see whether Jace would come back—that way led to brooding, then to craziness, and to her feral wolf coming out.

In shorts and a T-shirt, Deni planted new bedding flowers Will had brought home for her. The weather in Austin was usually dry enough and warm enough for her to mix arid climate plants like autumn sage with wetter weather plants like petunias and roses. Many Shifters went in for gardening, keeping their small yards colorful throughout the year. An antidote, Deni figured, to the restlessness that made them want to roam and fight. Nesting as compensation, she supposed.

Deni was straightening up from clipping off a few dead red roses when warmth covered her from behind.

"I prefer a sarong," Jace said, his breath hot in her ear.

"Do you?" Deni nestled back into him. "I'll get you one for yourself, then. Bet you'd look cute in it."

His laugh started all kinds of fires inside her. Deni turned in his arms, still holding her pruning scissors. She started to smile at him, but she broke off, seeing the streak of blood on the side of his neck.

"Are you all right?"

Jace moved the collar of his jacket over the wound. "Price of wisdom. We won't know what removing the Collars will do until we remove them."

"It's still on." Deni pointed at the Celtic cross at the hollow of his throat. Her bracelet, which she liked to wear as often as she could, clinked lightly against the cross. Deni's mother had left her the bracelet, a reminder of happier days.

"Baby steps. I think the Morrissey boys are through torturing me for the day, or at least the morning."

Deni touched her own Collar. "Do they really think they can get them off? I wonder if ..."

Jace closed his fingers over her hand as she started to tug at her Collar. "If taking yours off will stop your episodes? I don't want you risking that, Den. What they just did to me hurt like hell. I don't want you going through it until they know what they're doing."

Deni squeezed his hand. "Why are *you* going through it, then? I don't want you hurting like hell either."

Jace shrugged. "Someone needs to go first. Why not me?"

"Why should it be you?" she asked indignantly. "Let Liam and Sean torture themselves."

"Think about it." Jace laced his fingers through Deni's. "Sean's the Guardian. Liam's the Shiftertown leader. Dylan needs to be intact in case Liam needs backup. Connor their nephew is too young for this kind of pain. Liam's trackers—Ronan, Spike, Ellison—are mated now, with little ones, or little ones on the way. I'm a strong enough Shifter to take the experiment, and if something irreversible happens to me, my dad and my aunt Cass are already running our Shiftertown. I'm unmated, have no cubs ..."

"Meaning you're expendable?" Deni snatched her hand away, anger rising from someplace deep. "No one's expendable, Jace."

Jace gave her a tolerant look. "You're nice to worry about me. Now, how about putting on the sarong?"

Deni made a noise of exasperation and smacked at him with her empty hand. Jace caught her hand again and tugged her closer, up against his hard body.

His face lost its teasing expression, and his grip tightened. "Deni, you make me glad to be alive."

She looked up into his eyes, which held fire, and something in her that she hadn't realized was tight unwound itself.

Deni spread her fingers on his chest. "Don't let them have it all their own way."

Jace gave her a startled look as though surprised at her defense of him. He leaned down and kissed her, drawing the fire that had already begun inside her. He rested his cheek against hers after that, rocking a little as he held her, warmth to warmth.

Jace lifted his head, brushing Deni's hair from her face. "I'm beat. Too bad. I was hoping to do other things this morning."

The light in his eyes was suggestive, but he did look tired. Exhausted. He hadn't had much sleep in the night, and he'd been gone at dawn. Deni was willing to bet he hadn't eaten anything either.

"Take a load off," she said, gesturing to the porch. "Let me finish here, and I'll make a late breakfast. Or early lunch. Whatever you want to call it."

Jace gave her a smile and kissed her forehead, tightening his grip on her again, but finally he let her go. "Liam and Sean went home to consume a boatload of Guinness," he said, moving to the porch. He shook his head. "Irishmen."

He laughed, but Deni grew irritated. Liam expected Jace to sit still while he and Sean poked at him, and then they didn't even bother to feed him.

She jerked on her gardening gloves as the porch swing creaked—Jace let out a sigh as he relaxed on it—and went back to her task of spreading mulch around her new plants. A few roses to deadhead, and then she'd go whip up a mountain of eggs and a stack of bacon. Ellison would be up soon too, and she knew how much male Shifters loved to eat.

A small car pulled up across the street. Deni straightened to watch as Kim Morrissey descended in a neat skirt and blouse with low-heeled shoes. Deni sensed other

Shifters in yards and on porches down the street coming alert, watching too.

Kim looked over and gave Deni a brief wave, but her usual smiles were gone, her face set in grim lines. The passenger door had opened as Kim got out, and Dylan emerged.

Deni let out a breath of relief. Dylan was safe. She sensed the other Shifters relax as well, and saw them turn back to their morning tasks.

Dylan glanced at Deni then walked swiftly across the road toward Deni's yard. He paused at the edge of the browning grass, too much a Shifter to invade Ellison's territory without invitation. He only continued toward Deni at her flowerbed when she gave him a nod.

Dylan looked terrible. His cheeks were covered with black stubble, the gray that brushed his temples more prevalent this morning. His face was lined with dirt, his hair lank, his clothes smelling of stale smoke and sweat.

"You all right?" Dylan asked her.

"I should be asking *you* that," Deni said, pulling off her dirty gloves and dropping them to the ground. Dylan's blue eyes were always difficult to look into, but Deni met his gaze for a few beats.

"I'm good," Dylan said, though it was obvious he wasn't. He put a firm hand on Deni's shoulder and pulled her into a hug. "You did well last night, lass," he said. His arms tightened, the alpha giving one of his frightened Shifters reassurance.

A growl sounded. Low and vicious, it rolled out from the shadows, its threat clear.

Dylan jerked around, releasing Deni. An answering

growl came from his throat, Dylan too tired to worry about any kind of protocol. A Shifter threatened him—Dylan was going to strike him down.

It took Deni a second to realize that the rumble had come from Jace on the porch. He was still sitting on the porch swing, but alert, upright, his eyes glinting in the shadows.

Shifters in another's territory were always careful about what they did—this entire Shiftertown was technically Morrissey clan territory, though they respected the rights and privacy of individual families, packs, and prides. But a Shifter from out of town couldn't threaten, challenge, or cause any problems when he was an invited guest. It wasn't polite, and it was dangerous besides.

So why the hell was Jace Warden leaning forward, his gaze fast on Dylan, growling with full menace and ready to attack?

CHAPTER SIX

D*on't touch her,* Jace's growl said.

He knew Dylan understood him, because Dylan was staring back at Jace with full comprehension. Dylan was also angry, the short fuse of his temper not helped by his night in jail.

Jace knew he was violating all kinds of protocol, but he didn't give a crap. Dylan had put his hands on Deni, and Jace had seen her first.

A faint, logical voice deep inside Jace told him Dylan's reassurance of Deni was natural, and the intruder in this picture was Jace.

Jace kicked at the voice until it shut up. He knew if he rose from the swing, there'd be a fight, and he wasn't sure he wouldn't welcome it. If Dylan was a good Shifter and went along home, Jace would let him go. Otherwise ...

Dylan started for the porch. Jace recognized the determination in his stride, having seen it in his own father often enough. Dylan was coming to teach the upstart Jace a lesson.

Jace held his place on the porch swing. The logical voice had just enough volume to tell him that no one in this Shiftertown would take his side in a fight against Dylan. Not in a real one. This wasn't the fight club—fight club rules didn't apply here.

Dylan was on the steps, moving slowly but menacingly. Jace saw a flash out of the corner of his eye, and then Deni was leaping from the ground, up and over the porch railing with Lupine grace. The fact that she'd crushed one of her newly planted petunias as she made the vault told Jace of her apprehension.

Deni moved swiftly in front of Jace, facing Dylan before he reached the porch floor.

"He's tired and hurt," Deni said to Dylan, words coming fast. "Like you are. Let it go."

True, Jace was. But he was also enraged. A fight with Dylan would be fun. Lion against leopard—brute strength against finesse. Which would prevail?

Dylan looked at Deni, willing her to move. Deni held her ground. Good for her. Dylan growled a little, then he looked around Deni to Jace, his blue eyes going Shifter white.

"Den is right," Dylan said, every word slow and deliberate. He was holding himself back from throwing Deni aside and going for Jace, and making it clear he was holding back. "We're both exhausted." Dylan's gaze went to Jace's neck, where Jace's jacket had slid back again to reveal the loosened Collar link. "And you're in pain. Eat something. Sleep it off."

"Good advice," Deni said to Dylan. "Take it yourself. Neither of you got much sleep last night."

Jace remained silent, but he gave Dylan a slow nod. Dylan rested his gaze on Jace for a few moments longer, the weight of his stare palpable, before he turned and walked off the porch. He said nothing, not a good-bye or an acknowledgment, only strode away and back across the street to where Kim waited anxiously.

Deni watched Dylan go, her hands on her shapely hips. Jace could reach up and clasp those hips, pulling her back to his lap.

Deni swung around before he could move. "Are you all right? Why in the Goddess's name did you do that?"

Jace shrugged, which rubbed his jacket against his sore neck. "I didn't like the way he touched you."

"He's Shiftertown leader." Deni folded her arms and glared down at him. "It's his job to reassure us all, to make sure everyone's okay."

"He's not leader anymore."

"Not technically, no. But Liam still relies on him pretty heavily to keep the peace. Didn't Dylan invite you here in the first place?"

"He did." Jace knew everything Deni said was true and reasonable. But the mating frenzy only knew *mate* and *stay away from my mate.*

Time to apologize, make amends, tell Dylan he didn't mean to be an idiot. But Jace didn't want to. He still hurt from Liam's knife and Sean's soldering iron, and he needed a break.

Jace pressed his hands to his thighs and rose to his feet. He liked that Deni didn't take a step back but remained in his personal space, as though she belonged there.

"We're both tired," Jace said. "Like you said. Now, about this breakfast. Let's get something started. I'm *starving*."

———

Deni watched Jace eat. And eat, and eat. She put away a plate of eggs, bacon, and Texas toast herself, but Jace kept shoveling it in. Ellison woke up and joined them, as hungry as Jace.

"I guess no more fight club for a while," Ellison said after they discussed what had happened with the cops. "Damn. Shifters need to work off steam somehow or else we combust."

"You can work off steam by cleaning out the gutters and fixing the roof," Deni said, piling more eggs, cheese, and salsa onto both males' plates. "That will cool you down."

Jace laughed out loud. He was sweet and sexy, filling up the place at the table as though he belonged there.

Ellison grimaced. "Don't be so literal, woman."

"Just giving you an alternative," Deni said, resuming her seat. Jace closed his hand over hers, squeezing it, before he returned to his food. "I wouldn't want you to burst into flames."

Ellison looked over Jace and Deni, his gray eyes shrewd. He didn't pretend not to notice the signals between them, how comfortable they were sitting close together.

A knock sounded on the back door, and Jace came instantly alert. His hand jerked on Deni's, his eyes losing their deep greenness for a lighter hue.

At the same time a police car went by the house, its black body and white doors sliding past in silence. Ellison went noiselessly for the door and opened it to find a small boy with white hair and black eyes standing on the doorstep.

"Olaf," Ellison said, his body relaxing. "Maria's not home yet."

Maria often babysat for eleven-year-old Olaf, a polar bear cub, as well as other Shifter kids. She looked after them while their parents—or in Olaf's case, foster parents—worked.

"Ronan sent me to tell you the police are here," Olaf said.

"We see that." Ellison turned to watch a second car go past the front windows.

"They're going door-to-door," Olaf said. "Checking ID." He looked past Ellison and into the kitchen at Jace. "Everyone's ID."

Deni's heartbeat sped in alarm. "Does Ronan know if they're looking for someone in particular?"

Olaf shook his head. "No. They're just asking for ID." He peered at Jace, his small face blank. "What's the matter with him?"

"Nothing," Deni said quickly. "Long night."

Olaf didn't nod. He kept staring at Jace, his brow puckering. "He's not right."

With that declaration, Olaf turned from the door and

ran in a loping stride down the porch steps and across the backyard to the next house.

Ronan had been smart to send him as an early warning system, Deni thought as Ellison closed the door. If the police stopped him, all Olaf had to do was look cute and innocent, and charm them senseless. He did that so well.

Ellison came back to the kitchen, his shoulders tight. "Don't we have a new Shifter Bureau liaison to prevent this kind of harassment? I need to have a talk with Tiger."

"Maybe it's coming from a different department," Deni said. "Not our biggest concern at the moment."

Both she and her brother turned to look at Jace.

"Shit," Ellison said. Deni waited, tense. They could help Jace, but only if Ellison agreed.

Jace held up his hands. "I promise not to touch anything."

Ellison went past Deni and into the hall between kitchen, living room, and bedrooms. "Shit," he said again, his Texas accent thickening.

"No choice," Deni said to Ellison as she and Jace followed. "He doesn't have time to get away."

Ellison put his hand on the false wall panel in the middle of the hall. "You know this is a sacred trust," he said to Jace. "Right?"

"I'm familiar with the concept," Jace said impatiently.

"Damn it," Ellison said under his breath. "If I still had a pack, they'd kill me."

"I *am* your pack," Deni said. "And I'll speak for my sons. Jace goes to ground."

Were Jace anyone else, Deni would be as reluctant as

Ellison to open the door behind the paneling and let Jace see what was in there. But this was Jace, and she'd let him soothe her in the darkness at the fight club last night. He'd kept her from going feral, had gotten her home safely, and proved she could start going back to her normal life without fear. She owed him.

The opening door revealed a set of cement stairs heading down into darkness. The three of them paused at the top a moment, letting the air from below cool them.

Secret spaces. Every Shifter house had them. Traditionally built below the main house, they held secrets of that Shifter pack or clan, things collected and cherished, the pack's wealth. Shifters had survived all these centuries because of the things contained in their vaults. Shifters now lived together aboveground in relative peace—different clans and species rubbing elbows, or paws—because they kept this part of themselves, places only close family went, safely underground.

To let an unrelated Shifter see the secret spaces was unthinkable. Jace wasn't family or clan—he wasn't even Lupine.

Another knock came, this one on the front door, and much firmer than Olaf's. "Mr. Rowe?" a man's voice sounded.

Ellison let out a growl and headed for the front. Jace, instead of going down the stairs, spun and started after him, stepping in front of Deni as though protecting her.

"No!" Deni whispered. She grabbed Jace by the jacket and shook him. "Get down there."

Jace swung around and gave her a startled look, as

though he'd had no idea he'd gone into his protective stance. His eyes were the light green again, his Shifter rage apparent.

Deni knew he didn't want to go down the stairs without her, to leave her vulnerable. But this wasn't the wild. This was the human world, and at the moment, she and Jace had to play by their rules, or risk everything.

"Down," Deni whispered again.

Jace finally nodded, let her push him to the first stair, and held her gaze as she shut the door on him. Deni had the false panel back in place and was walking out toward the living room by the time two police officers, one armed with a tranq rifle, strode in and demanded to see her and Ellison's IDs.

———

Jace remained in the stairwell, pressing his fists to the stone wall, dragging in deep breaths. He knew he couldn't risk the police finding him, but the need to keep them away from Deni had risen swiftly, his primal fear for her driving away common sense.

He could hear the police through the thin paneling, talking to Ellison and Deni, asking where Maria was, and about Deni's sons. Human hearing wasn't as good as Shifters', but Jace knew they might be able to hear any noise he made if he wasn't careful.

In silence, he walked the rest of the way down the stairs, his Feline eyes letting him see in the dark. At the bottom was a door, unlocked. Jace opened it as noiselessly as he could, slipped inside the basement room, and closed the door behind him.

Only then did he flip one of the switches beside the door, only one. A single light came on in the middle of the room.

Jace looked around. *Nice.* The main room held soft-looking furniture and opened to a kitchen larger than the one upstairs, with more upscale appliances. The refrigerator was stocked, he saw when he opened it. A Shifter could live down here comfortably for weeks.

A flat screen TV had been mounted to a wall, and a game console and controls sat under it. Jace smiled. Will and Jackson must have fun down here. Probably Ellison too. Deni likely held her own. Why Shifters liked to play RPGs, Jace had never figured out—they were shapeshifters and fighters in real life—but given the opportunity to take a new identity and kick a troll's ass, they couldn't resist.

Games were off-limits right now. Jace couldn't risk that the humans upstairs wouldn't hear. Shifter spaces were usually soundproofed, but soundproofing was only so good.

Jace figured Ellison would want Jace to stand with his eyes closed in the middle of the room and not smell, see, or touch anything. And then somehow wipe his memory of everything the moment he left. He had to smile.

In any other situation, Jace might try to keep clear of the Rowe family's secrets. But this was Deni's place. It held the essence of her, even more than the house upstairs did.

Jace couldn't resist stopping by the tall cabinet that held books and a collection of framed photographs. Family photos. A tall couple Jace didn't recognize must be Ellison and Deni's parents. The photo was old, but kept with care.

Another older photo showed Deni, much younger, probably just past her Transition, with a male Shifter. The Shifter male, who had black hair and gray eyes, was a Lupine, big and rawboned, like most of the wolves. Deni leaned against him, a smile on her face, looking happy.

Deni's name was still Rowe, Jason mused. She hadn't taken her mate's family's name, which meant her mate had been of lesser dominance than her, probably much less. These days, it was a female's choice which name to take, but in the past, that choice had been made for her by whichever family was dominant. Even now, more domi-nant families would fight to keep their daughters under their name. Deni had been mated long ago enough that she'd likely gone along with the tradition.

Another picture of Deni showed her holding two wolf cubs, the pair bright-eyed. Will and Jackson, as pups. Deni's mate must have taken the photo, because Deni smiled out of the picture at him, her eyes full of love.

More recent photos showed Deni with Will and Jackson as tall young men, all of them wearing Collars. Then one of Ellison cuddling the small human woman, Maria, both grinning. Ellison wore a more relaxed expres-sion than Jace had ever seen on him.

Another was of Deni alone. The river was in the back-ground, Deni in a bathing suit and wrap, her hair wet, the gold bracelet she liked to wear on her wrist. She smiled with all the animation she'd showed when she'd held her cubs. This was Deni happy, without the haunted look in her eyes. Before the accident, Jace figured.

A sudden savage fury rose up in him, filling his throat with growls. She'd been deliberately run down by a human trying to kidnap her. Though the man had been killed, Jace wanted the culprit in front of him, so he could have the pleasure of ripping his head off.

His rage rose so quickly that he started to shift. Then his Collar shocked him.

The pain was fierce. Jace dug his fist into his mouth to cut off the scream that had welled up, ready to burst out.

Son of a bitch. He closed his eyes, trying to breathe, rapidly repeating the meditation mantra to calm the Collar. The Collar shocked him again, and he balled his hands in agony.

What the fuck?

Jace found himself on the floor, arms curled around his legs as he rocked in pain. Flashes of rage went through him, followed by just as intense flashes of need. Need for Deni.

He needed her touch, her kiss, to breathe her scent. Her body against his. Another time of passion with her, another time when he'd bury himself inside her and be, for once in his life, complete.

"Shit," he said out loud.

This wasn't mating frenzy. Or maybe it partly was.

But Jace recognized his symptoms from seeing them in an unfortunate few. Rabid hunger. Intense need for sex. Quick to anger, ready to kill, especially to protect what was his.

Only two links of his Collar had been pulled away, not even that, but it had triggered the feral in him.

Shouldn't surprise him, he reflected. Liam had said

taking off the Collars made the instincts suppressed by years of wearing them burst out in a volcanic flare. The trick would be figuring out how to negate the effect.

For now, Jace had to control himself. Somehow. The police upstairs were interrogating the woman he wanted. But he couldn't think about that. If he did, he'd rush up there and destroy them all.

Keep it together.

Funny, it had been easy to tell Deni to keep herself calm. Difficult to convince himself to do so now.

Jace yanked open the door of the cabinet—he stopped himself from simply smashing the glass and putting his hand through it. He took out the photo of Deni by herself, smiling cheerfully out at him.

He touched her face with his fingers, drawing a deep breath. Looking at Deni kept him cool, but barely.

Jace had to know what was happening upstairs. Were they taking away Deni in a patrol car, arresting her for whatever reason?

He clutched the picture to his chest, trying to still his need to run up the stairs and drag Deni to safety. He had to *think.*

Jace was smart—he'd designed most of the underground space and its gadgets in the house he shared with his dad and family in the Vegas Shiftertown. He'd been recruited to design the spaces in the new houses being built out there as well. What had he done to make sure they wouldn't get trapped in their own hiding places, without knowing what was going on in the outside world?

He moved to the TV, made sure the sound was all the way down, and clicked it on. A little button pushing on the remote ... Yes, they'd done it too. Or maybe they'd followed Jace's design, which Eric liked to brag about.

One of the TV channels monitored the upstairs. Ellison must have put cameras in the big living room and one on the front porch. They focused now, showing Deni standing next to Ellison, both she and her brother upright but easy, without defiance.

Four cops barred their way out of the room, the female one with the tranq rifle talking to them. Ellison and Deni answered, standing casually, trying not to betray nervousness through body language. Humans were not as good at reading nonverbal signals as Shifters, but some could be good at it, especially the police sent to deal with Shifters.

Jace inched up the volume, but the sound was too muffled for him to make out what they were saying. No one was lunging to put Ellison or Deni in cuffs, fortunately. Just cops talking to citizens, citizens who happened to be Shifters.

Jace sat down on the couch, unwilling to look away. He hugged Deni's picture to him almost without realizing it. He was still hugging it when the cops finally left the house and Deni came downstairs to find him.

———

JACE WAS OFF THE COUCH AND AT THE BOTTOM OF THE stairs as soon as Deni stepped off them. Deni found herself caught in a hard hug, Jace lifting her from her feet.

"It's all right, Jace," she said quickly. "I'm all right."

Jace growled and buried his face in her neck. Deni

held him, the solidness of his body against hers slowing her racing heart.

"You touched stuff," Ellison said, half joking. He went past Jace, snatched the remote off the couch, and clicked off the television. He started to close the cabinet door and stopped. "You touched more stuff."

Deni took the framed photo of herself from Jace's hand. She had to tug at it before he blinked and let it go, as though he'd forgotten he was clutching it so tightly. Deni handed it to Ellison, who restored it to the cabinet, not before giving Jace a sharp look.

"Did you hear what they said?" Deni asked.

"Not well." Jace released her from the hug and took a firm hold of her hand. "I only saw they didn't arrest you, thank the Goddess. What happened?"

"They're interested in what Shifters have been up to lately," Ellison said. "*Very* interested. Looking at identification, asking where we're working, what we're doing when we're not."

"Have to wonder why they're asking all the sudden," Jace said. "Right after I arrived. I don't believe in coincidences."

"Neither do I." Ellison and Jace shared a grim look. "I hate to say this, but you'd better stay down here awhile. They're roving Shiftertown, and probably won't be leaving soon."

Deni saw the flash in Jace's eyes, the wild look she saw in herself sometimes. *Trapped.*

She touched his arm. "I'll stay here with you."

Jace's look changed in an instant to something hungry and raw, his eyes going very light green. "You shouldn't."

"You're hurting." Deni put her fingers to the red marks around his Collar but she didn't touch them. "Because of this?"

"I don't know." Jace's hand was sweating, slick against hers. "I think so."

"I knew Liam was crazy," Ellison said. "Going on about releasing us from Collars. I'm going to go get Dylan, have him look in on you."

"Be careful," Deni said.

Ellison tipped an imaginary cowboy hat. "I'm always careful, ma'am," he drawled, then went past them and up the stairs.

"Let's sit down." Deni started to lead Jace to the sofa, but he didn't budge. His body was strong, a boulder she couldn't move.

"Den, you should get out of here." His grip was tight, his hand hot.

Deni's heart beat faster as she touched his wrist and found his pulse banging beneath her fingers. "I think I should stay. Ellison will be right back."

"No, *go!*" Jace pushed at her, his breath coming fast. "If you stay, I don't know what I'll do. I want you—last night wasn't enough. I want it hard, and I want it now. Don't let me take it from you."

Deni let go of his hand, but she remained squarely in front of him. A Shifter going feral and feeling mating frenzy was a dangerous thing. Jace could do anything, even kill her, if he was crazed enough. She understood that.

On the other hand, in mating frenzy, only the mate kept a Shifter from completely losing his mind. She thought of Jace behind her on the motorcycle, warming her and giving her the strength to cut through her fears and get them home. He'd been with her every second, and he'd held her in victory when she'd made it. When Jace had to hide down here, Deni had reasoned that she owed him. She still believed that.

"I'm not leaving," she said.

Jace's eyes turned all the way white. He grabbed Deni by the wrists and hauled her against him.

CHAPTER SEVEN

Deni landed against Jace's chest, his skin hot through his thin shirt. His jacket's zipper rubbed Deni's arms, the friction of it releasing the heat in her own body.

Jace's kiss was hard, opening her mouth, his grip on her wrists crushing. But Deni was strong, had always been strong. She could not have endured so much without strength. She rose on her tiptoes, kissing him back, her body fitting to his.

Jace raised his head, breaking the kiss. His lips were parted, the moisture inside his mouth beckoning her. Deni knew his taste now and craved more. She also knew what he felt like inside her, and she wanted that again. She wanted his firm body on top of hers, wanted the heat of his thrusts to fill her. Deni reached for the button of his jeans and slid it open.

Jace tightened his fingers on her wrist again. "Don't play with fire."

"I'm cold," Deni said in a low voice. "Warm me up."

Jace was struggling with coherence. "Ellison will be back soon, you said."

She gave him a hot smile. "Then we should hurry."

"Bloody hell."

Deni unzipped his jeans. He hadn't bothered with underwear this morning, she found as she dipped her hand inside. His cock, hard and hot, tumbled into her hand.

Jace let out a groan. He jerked Deni against him, his arm solidly behind her as she lightly stroked him. "Gods, woman."

"You woke me up, Jace," she said. "I want to thank you for that."

"In the middle of last night, you mean?" His words were strained. "I was feeling payback from the fight. Tried to keep it quiet."

"You know I don't mean that." Deni squeezed his cock until he let out another noise of pleasure.

"*Damn.*" Jace tugged her hand from him but only to lift her into his arms, kissing her with a ferocity that tasted of fire.

The sofa was near. Jace tipped Deni back over its arm until they both fell onto its cushions, arms and legs bumping and tangling in each other's. Deni laughed.

The laughter probably saved her, she thought later. Jace shook his head slightly as though clearing his mind, and his eyes took on a jade hue again. He slowed his kisses to something tender, lips soft on Deni's. She ran her fingers through the short ends of his hair, liking the warm brush of it.

Jace unbuttoned her shorts, tugging them down and off with a contortion of bodies that had them laughing again. His jeans landed on the floor on top of the shorts, and then they were body to body. Deni took handfuls of his jacket, but before she could start to coax it off, Jace slid inside her.

All the way in. Last night had been wild and fast, a raw coupling at the edge of a parking lot. Now everything stopped. Jace looked into Deni's eyes, the feral Shifter softening into a man, hard-faced but warm-eyed.

He filled her, his breath slowing as he lay on her, touching her face. The pressure of him inside her loosened her entire body, and Deni wrapped herself around him, drawing him in.

Jace closed his eyes, letting out another soft moan. He kissed her mouth, giving a nip to the corner of it.

After a moment, he opened his eyes again and started to move. Slow thrusts, intensity building as each one completed. Jace held her gaze, his eyes a dark green now. The frenzied animal had calmed. Now it was just Deni and Jace.

Deni arched under him, Jace's thrusts coming faster. Her back pressed into the sofa's soft foam cushions, all the way down to the springs. She held him close, laughing into his hair as the springs started to squeak.

"Goddess, you are beautiful," Jace whispered, feathering kisses over her face. "I came here to find you; I know I did."

He'd been to this Shiftertown before, but Deni knew what he meant. They'd been ready to meet last night.

The soft fleece of Jace's jacket felt good to Deni's hands, the zipper rough against her palms. As he kissed her, she could again see where one link of his Collar and part of another had been taken off, his skin angry red beneath.

He'd been ready to kill Dylan on the porch, and the police when they'd knocked on the door. The loosening Collar was letting out his feral instincts, she guessed. Liam had explained to her when she'd first considered trying to take her Collar off that such a thing might happen. But for now, Jace gentled himself, loving her without madness.

He kept thrusting, and Deni moved under him, meeting those thrusts. His jacket held his heat, and she slid her hands into it, finding his hard back beneath. Jace's honed body was sleek under her touch, the lithe dance of his muscles exciting.

They were both breathing hard, uttering little groans, holding on to each other when heavy footsteps sounded on the other side of the couch.

A pair of brawny fists jammed to the back of the sofa, and Deni looked up in time to see Ellison spin away in half disgust, half irritation. "Are you kidding me?" Ellison growled.

Jace said, "Shit," and the feral whiteness returned to his eyes. He was up off the sofa, his jacket falling, but it wasn't long enough to hide his privates. Deni saw his cock, still dark and hard from what they'd been doing, black hair crisp at its base.

Deni knew Dylan was upstairs, away from their basement sanctuary, of course. Ellison kept his back squarely turned. That back was quivering, but Deni couldn't tell whether from rage or laughter. A little of both, probably.

"Goddess, Den, he's a *Feline*," Ellison said. He shook his head without turning around, the overhead light gleaming in his blond hair. "Both of you get your asses upstairs. *After* you've covered them."

He gave one more shake of his head and started for the steps. His cowboy boots grated on the cement stairs, then he was gone.

Deni swallowed, tamping down her need to burst into hysterical laughter. "I guess he was faster than I thought he'd be."

Jace didn't smile. "He needs to respect you."

Deni sat up, pushing her hair from her face. "He just caught you making the beast with two backs with his little sister. Give him a break."

Jace growled again, then he reached down and helped Deni to her feet. As she came off the couch, he pulled her against him. "You all right?"

"Yes." Deni truly was. She should be embarrassed at being caught by her brother—at being reckless like this. But she wasn't. It seemed natural to be coupling with Jace. Shifters celebrated sex, because it meant life, cubs, continuance. She wouldn't apologize for it.

"What about you?" Deni asked. Jace was shaking, but his hold on her was strong.

"I'll be okay." Jace took a long breath and pulled her into a tighter hug. His bare cock touched her abdomen. "I get it now—what you must go through when you start losing track of who you are. I shouldn't have made light of it."

Deni looked up at him in alarm. "Are you losing track of who you are?"

"Not quite." Jace kissed her hair and rested his cheek

on the top of her head. "But almost. You keep reminding me who I am, though, all right?"

———

"They're looking for someone," Dylan said when they emerged upstairs.

They spoke in the kitchen, where the windows were high, small, curtained, and looked out to the backyard. The wide windows of the bungalow's living room were out of bounds.

Jace didn't like human police roving Shiftertown, but right now, his body hummed from the nearness of Deni, and the remembered joy of being in her one more time.

He loved the sweetness of her scent, today coupled with fresh earth from her digging in the dirt. The taste of her filled him like heady wine. He was imprinted with her now, the feel of her soft thighs against his legs, the way she squeezed him when he pressed inside her.

"Jace?" Deni said.

She wasn't trying to get his attention, he realized after a heartbeat. She was asking Dylan if Jace was the Shifter the police were looking for.

"They didn't say," Dylan answered. "I don't even know if they're looking for a Shifter. They had a tip-off, I got one of the officers to tell me, about the fight club. I told them there's always rumors of a Shifter fight club, because humans find it titillating. Same as rumors of Shifter hookers."

Shifter women never sold sex, never had. But Shifter women could be promiscuous, because Shifters didn't find sex shameful. As long as a Shifter was unmated, they could have as many partners as they wanted. Not all liked to go roaming, but some Shifter women spread it around. Humans confused that with the sex trade. Hence, the rumors.

"Tip-off from a human?" Ellison asked.

"They wouldn't tell me that." Dylan's eyes glinted. "What Shifter would betray us?"

Ellison shrugged. "One pissed off for some reason. At other Shifters, or at you. Broderick springs to mind."

"He sprang to my mind too. I'll be having a talk with him." Dylan's Irish accent made the words sound casual, but Jace heard the steel behind them.

"If they're going door-to-door, what about the workshop?" Jace asked.

Dylan shook his head. "They haven't found it yet. Lie low here, and I'll send for you when it's clear. If it is." Dylan looked Jace up and down. "We might want to stop the experiment anyway. It's affecting you."

"Agreed," Deni said quickly.

Jace shook his head. "No, we'll never get the Collars off by being afraid to have them off. I want to keep at it." It was tempting to turn his back on the agony, and Sean with his soldering iron, and run for home, but learning all they could about the Collars was too important. Besides, Deni was here.

"We'll see." Dylan gave him another hard look. Jace knew his display on the porch had not won him any favors from Dylan, but Jace had definitely not liked Dylan touching Deni, even innocently.

"Why did you want me to meet you at the fight club?"

Jace asked him. "I could have come to Shiftertown and waited for you."

Dylan's face shuttered. "For reasons that are no longer important. Don't leave this house until I let you know it's all right. Catch up on sleep or something." Dylan glanced from Jace to Deni. "I mean real sleep."

Jace didn't bother to answer. Deni went pink, but only because Ellison was rolling his eyes.

———

Ellison agreed that Jace could stay downstairs until Dylan gave the all clear. Safer, he said, in case the cops tried to surprise them. Police had been known to walk right into Shifter houses, the rules about warrants being a little relaxed when Shifters were concerned.

Deni was glad Ellison shared her worry for Jace, though Ellison was a bit grumpy about it. Finding Jace and Deni in flagrante hadn't been the highlight of his day, he said.

"It's not like I've never come home to you and Maria in the living room," Deni reminded him.

Ellison gave her an innocent look. "That's different."

"My ass," Deni said, sending him a smile.

"I know it was, and I don't want to see it again," Ellison said. "Or Jace's. Yetch."

At least he was teasing now, even if he was annoyed.

When Will and Jackson returned home, Ellison apprised them of the situation. Maria, now growing plump with Ellison's first cub, was home by that time too. She was taking classes at a community college in preparation for entering the university next year and spent the rest of her day taking care of Shifter cubs. Maria had lost the haunted look she'd worn since she'd been rescued, and Ellison had lost his look of deep loneliness. Now if Deni could just lose hers.

They played video games in the basement, Jace proving to be very good at them. Will, who was turning out to be a computer genius, had a hard time keeping up with him.

Deni worried that the games might start drawing out Jace's feral anger, but they didn't. Maybe knowing it wasn't real, only pixels on a screen, made a difference. Deni was never upset by the games either. But then, games had no scent, no texture. Shifters were more stimulated by things that assaulted all the senses at once.

By the time Will and Jackson went to bed, they'd expressed more respect for Jace. He might be twenty years older, but his knowledge of games and computer programming helped him rise in their estimation.

Before Deni could start arguing with Ellison that she wanted to stay downstairs and sleep with Jace, Sean arrived at the back door to tell them the police had gone, had been for several hours.

"But we wanted to wait until we were certain," Sean said, lounging against the kitchen doorframe, his sword gleaming under the porch light. "Didn't want them doubling back and saying *just fooling*." He glanced at Jace, who stood behind Ellison, Jace conceding Ellison's place to guard the house. "You ready for more torture, lad?"

"You're not going to do more tonight, are you?" Deni asked sharply. "Leave Jace alone. He needs to rest."

"Liam wants to continue under cover of darkness," Sean said. "We'll leave sleeping for the day. Felines are mostly nocturnal anyway, lass."

"It's all right," Jace said. "I want to finish this." He looked less crazed—maybe gaming did have a good effect on the mind. "Liam's waiting there?"

"Liam's at the bar, as usual, in case whoever is calling in tip-offs reports any out-of-the-ordinary activity. Me and Dad will be working on you tonight. Plus a little extra help." Sean looked at Ellison. "Liam says you and Maria are to go to the bar. Laugh it up, talk to your friends, have fun. You too, Deni."

"Nope." Deni took a step closer to Jace. "I'm going with him. You Morrisseys are too eager to dig knives into him. Someone needs to be there who's on his side."

Sean lifted both hands and didn't argue. Of the two Morrissey brothers—much alike with their dark hair and blue eyes—Sean was the more easygoing. If Deni wanted to throw her lot in with Jace, Sean was saying, who was he to stop her?

Ellison wasn't happy to let Deni go to the workshop, but Maria took Deni's side, saying she wouldn't let Ellison go alone if she had to make the same kind of choice. The ladies prevailed, to Deni's satisfaction.

They left the house together, Ellison and Maria breaking away to walk to the bar, Ellison's arm firmly around Maria's waist. Sean and Deni put Jace between them, with Jace walking in the hunched manner he'd been taking on, the hood of his jacket up to hide most of his face.

Deni caught a whiff of a strange scent when they approached the workshop's door, one that had her hackles rising. The wolf in her was growling, and she felt the bite of nausea that was a prelude to her losing herself. She clutched Jace's arm, and he stepped away from Sean to her.

"What is it, sweetheart?"

"There's someone ..."

"I know," Jace said. "I smell it."

It was an acrid odor, one ripe with ancestral memory.

Sean said, "No worries. That will be the father-in-law," and he ushered them inside.

CHAPTER EIGHT

Jace stepped into the room and faced a strange apparition. A tall man, so tall he looked stretched, turned toward them, a metallic whisper sounding as he moved. He was dressed in chain mail, which was covered with a cloak so black it was like an opening into darkness.

The man's hair, in contrast, was pale white, and fell in dozens of braids past his waist, but the effect wasn't effeminate, nor was he elderly. The man's face was sharp, his dark eyes rivaling his cloak for the deepest hue of black. He wore a broadsword on his back, one larger than the Sword of the Guardian, its hilt sticking up above his head.

Deni was still growling, and Jace's snarls filled his throat. An ancient enemy stood before them, and though Jace had seen this man before on other trips to Austin, the shock of him being here made his wildcat a little crazy.

"You remember Fionn," Sean was saying. He eyed Jace

warily, as though ready to stop Jace's attack. "My mate's true father."

Andrea Morrissey, Sean's mate, appeared on the other side of the Fae, flanking him in a protective move. Andrea's dark head was up, her gray eyes daring Jace and Deni to do anything against Fionn.

Andrea was half Fae, half Shifter. Fionn, Jace had been told, had come to the human world forty or so years ago, seeking refuge during some unknown Fae war. He'd met and fallen in love with a Shifter woman, a Lupine, who'd then borne Andrea. For complicated Fae reasons, he hadn't been able to stay, and Andrea had been raised by her mother and a Shifter stepfather. Andrea had had it tough as a half Fae growing up among Shifters and hadn't met her true father until a few years ago Now Andrea was mate to the Guardian, and no one hassled her about her origins. Not to her face, anyway, and never within Sean's hearing.

Fionn had proved himself to be on the Shifters' side in many cases, but the sight of a Fae still made Jace want to shift, fight, and kill. The Fae had created the first Shifters many centuries ago, breeding them to be fighting slaves. The Shifters had finally broken away from their Fae captors, staying in the human world while the Fae retreated permanently to Faerie. The Shifter-Fae war had ended seven hundred years ago, but still Shifters had a tough time even looking at a Fae.

Jace cleared his throat. "I assume you came to help with the Collars?"

Fionn curled his lip—Fae were always prone to sneering. "No, I came for a barbeque. Haven't got my fill of Texas ribs." He turned his disdainful dark eyes to Sean. "Why you think I can help, I don't know. I'm a warrior, not a magician. I don't know anything about the Fae magic in these Collars."

Andrea put her hand on Fionn's arm. Fionn softened as he turned to his daughter—the only person Jace had ever seen Fionn be nice to.

"But you might have some insight into their construction," Andrea said. "It's Fae technology as well as Fae magic."

Fionn patted her hand. "We've had this discussion before. I don't know anything about what Fae did with Shifters. Shifters were out of Faerie, never to return, before I was born. I can see where Shifters would have been useful in battle, but I for one wouldn't want to put up with them between wars. I'd have to cage them up to keep them from killing me, and they'd cost a fortune to feed."

Deni made a growling noise in her throat. "Good thing we won the Shifter-Fae war, then." she said.

"Yes, good thing," Fionn answered. "Saved me a lot of bother."

Andrea shot Fionn a frown. "Sorry, my father enjoys baiting Shifters. He thinks it's *fun*."

"I may be looking for amusement in the situation, but I also speak the truth," Fionn said.

From what Jace understood, Fionn was a formidable warrior in his world, leading the armies of his clan in victory over other Fae, and possessing a lot of power. Other Fae had learned not to mess with him. Jace noted that

Fionn kept his eye on everything in the room, including all the exits, the high windows, and anything that could become a weapon . He might be here to help, but he couldn't stop being a fighter by instinct.

Dylan opened a locked cabinet and removed a silver and black chain. Jace recoiled inside, and he felt Deni move closer to him. Even Sean shivered. This was a true Collar, and Dylan carried it to Fionn.

"We're looking for the third element," Dylan said. "Fae magic, computer chips, and something else."

Fionn took the Collar gingerly between his fingers, held it up to his eye level, and scanned it. The small circle of the Celtic cross glittered in the harsh light of bare bulbs.

"Interesting." Fionn ran a fingertip down the links. "Silver and black silver, which is a Fae metal. No iron." If it had contained iron, Fionn couldn't have held it—iron made Fae sick, could even kill them if they had too much contact with it. Fionn looked the Collar over again, frowning. "Sorry, I don't know. My experience with metals is confined to swords and other bladed weapons. Not jewelry."

"Well," Sean said, letting out a disappointed sigh as Dylan took the Collar back, "let's see what we can do tonight."

He unsheathed the Sword of the Guardian again and laid it on the table. Jace thought Fionn would walk out, back to the circle of trees that took him to Faerie, but Fionn settled himself against the wall near Andrea and folded his arms, ready to watch.

"You did that before," Jace said to Sean, sitting on a

stool and trying to stem his nervousness. "Took out the sword before we started. Why?"

Sean shrugged. "I thought the magic in it might help figure out the magic in the Collars. Magic vibrations or something. The sword has done some interesting things." He glanced at Andrea, who nodded. The two together had performed amazing bouts of healing, when both of them had been touching the sword.

"Ready?" Sean asked Jace.

"No. But let's do this."

Dylan held the knife Liam had used, plus an electric probe, while Sean stuck with the soldering iron. Jace balled his fists, setting his teeth against the coming pain.

A soothing coolness cut through the heat in his body, originating at a point on his wrist. Opening eyes he hadn't realized he'd closed, Jace saw Deni's hand, tanned from the sun, resting on his forearm. She looked at him, giving him a little nod and smile, her gray eyes warm. An answering warmth stirred in Jace's heart, wrapping around his nerves and breaking through his fear of the pain.

"Hurry up, Sean," Jace said without taking his gaze from Deni. "Other things I want to do tonight."

"You got it, lad." Sean brought the soldering iron closer as Dylan touched the electric probe to Jace's Collar.

A vibrating buzz went around the chain, and then Jace felt the nick of the knife. The iron heated the silver, and the second link Liam had already loosened came free. Dylan quickly lifted a third, then a fourth.

The pain was there, but not as intense as last time. That is, until Dylan tried to loosen a fifth link. The Collar snapped back a huge arc that jolted Dylan backward and shocked hot pain into Jace. Deni jumped as well, caught in the current, but she didn't let go of Jace.

Jace tried to clench his teeth over his yell, to keep quiet, but his body had taken over. Darkness clamped his brain, and through it he saw the Collar, a white band around his neck, every nerve outlined with fire.

His yell turned to a scream. The Collar didn't want to let go of him. It clung tighter to Jace's neck, the link Dylan had just pulled off fusing again to his skin.

Jace fell from the stool to the floor, landing on his knees, brutal pain the only thing in his world. Every nerve was crackling, cold washing through him followed by heat so powerful he burned from the inside out. He started to shift, but every bit of fur emerging from his skin hurt, doubling his agony.

"Jace." Deni's voice cut through the fog. Her touch fell like cool water on his burning skin. "Hold on."

Jace heard other voices, too faint and faraway to bother with. "Shit." "Andrea, can you help him, lass?" "Have you killed him?" came Fionn's disdain. "Well done, Shifters."

The only important words were breathed in Deni's voice. "I'm here, Jace. Hang on."

Jace clung to her voice, needing its warm cadence. His brain couldn't form the syllables of her name, but it didn't matter. He knew her touch, her warmth as she put her arms around him, on her knees too. He knew her scent, the low sweetness of her voice, the soft gray of her eyes, which went a lighter gray when he made love to her. Jace took a long breath, taking in the goodness of her.

The hurting eased the slightest bit. Underneath the

pain, the tightness in Jace's chest radiated a different kind of tingling—it still hurt, but without the brutal sharpness of the Collar.

Jace held his breath, wondering if the second pressure was what he thought it was. Through pain came amazing happiness and at the same time dismay. *Not now. Not here. Wrong time. Wrong place.*

"Jace." The word cut through his agony.

Deni. She was Deni, lithe, beautiful. And a *Lupine*, for crying out loud. Their kids wouldn't know whether to bark or meow.

"Help me," he croaked.

Deni's warmth covered him, her breasts soft against his burning chest. "Hold on to me."

She had both his hands between hers, her head on his shoulder. The Collar kept sparking, biting into her as well. She took up the dregs of the pain, jumping a little as the sparks bit deep.

Another female hand touched Jace, this one inflicting a new kind of pain. His nerves balled into one place of fire, Jace shouting with it, then slowly, it eased.

Jace drew a long breath and opened his eyes.

He found himself flat on his back in the middle of a circle of faces—Andrea, Sean, Dylan, Fionn, Deni. Andrea had one hand on the blade of the Sword of the Guardian, which was humming. Fionn's long, thin braids brushed Jace's legs, Fionn's concern mixed with curiosity and fascination.

Deni raised her head and touched Jace's face, her little bracelet making a faint jingling noise. She exhaled in relief.

"Sorry, Jace," Sean said, his voice rumbling with sympathy. "You all right, lad?"

Jace opened his mouth to say he'd live, but nothing came out. He dropped his head back in exhaustion.

"Leave him be," Deni said, suddenly brisk. "Sean, hand me that blanket. You all have tortured him enough tonight."

Sweet of her to take care of him. Jace didn't move—mostly because he couldn't—and let himself enjoy Deni draping a thick blanket over him and lifting his head in her competent hand to slide a cushion underneath it.

She started to get her feet again, but Jace grabbed her hand. *No. Stay.*

Deni caught his gaze, her own filled with pain and worry. She gave him a nod and sank down beside him, folding her lovely legs under her.

"We need to find the link," Dylan said. "No use half killing him trying to pull any more off tonight."

"Agreed," Sean said, sounding relieved.

"If you pull it off all at once, he goes feral?" Fionn asked, sounding interested. The lilting accent in his voice, different from any Jace had ever heard, made him start to growl.

"Aye, that's what happens," Sean said. "Have seen it myself. If the Shifter is too far gone, he can't come back. Best you can do is kill the poor bugger."

Jace growled again. Deni held him tighter and kissed his lower lip. "I won't let them," she said.

Jace remained still. He didn't trust himself not to attack everyone in the room if he moved, with the exception of Deni. He might even go for Andrea, but only after he smacked down the Fae who stank up the place.

"Jace needs to rest," Deni said. "Leave him be."

"I know," Sean said, putting a hand on Jace's shoulder. He quickly took it away as Jace's growl turned to a snarl. "You take as long as you need, lad. We won't start again until you're ready."

"No, you'll find yourselves another victim," Deni said sharply. She sat up, but kept herself between Jace and the others.

"Not victim," Sean said. "Volunteer."

"I know what I said." Deni glared at them, Lupine defiance in the face of powerful Felines. What a sweetheart. "Leave him alone and figure out your problem with someone else. Like me, for instance. I'm already half crazy, so I might not notice the difference."

"No!" Jace came up off the floor to fold himself protectively around Deni. "No." He still had to think about how to form words. "Won't let you. Too much pain."

Deni gave him a startled look, then a stubborn one. "Well, I won't let them put *you* in too much pain either." She switched her anger back to Sean and Dylan. "He's not expendable."

Both Sean and Dylan took a step away, as though sensing something had changed about Deni, and about Jace. Andrea unfolded to her feet and turned to the sink to run some water. The Sword of the Guardian had cut her hand. Brave woman, saying nothing.

"Interesting how the female defends the male," Fionn said. "Fae women, on the other hand, can turn on their men in a heartbeat, running them through and joining their enemies if they find it expedient. Shifter females, I note, will stick with their mates even when the mate is defeated. She'll die for him."

"Isn't that what attracted you to my mother?" Andrea asked from the sink.

Fionn went silent a moment, and when he spoke again, the arrogance had gone from his voice and a sad note entered it. "Yes. One of the many things."

"Jace and Deni aren't mated," Sean said. He slid the Sword of the Guardian back into its scabbard and moved to Andrea as though drawn to her.

Fionn's arrogance returned. "And I'm constantly amazed at how dense Shifters are about their own kind."

"That's enough, Father," Andrea said firmly.

Jace pulled Deni back to him. He didn't care anymore about the Collars, about freeing Shifters, about helping Liam. He wanted Deni—wanted to bury himself in her and not come out. Whether she felt the same about him, Jace didn't know, but he would find out. If she didn't care about him, if he'd simply been a way for her to defuse pressure, he'd let her go.

The thought of letting Deni go made his feral side want to burst out again. Jace kissed her shoulder, drawing in her scent until it calmed him a bit.

This was the wrong time and place for a mate-claim. He wanted it to be special, right, with his family present, and hers as well. They were from two different Shifter-towns, which would be a problem, but they could work it out somehow.

After they figured out this stupid Collar situation, Jace would get official permission to visit and mate-claim Deni.

Deni could always turn him down, her choice, but Jace would take some time to persuade her.

He was busy thinking of fun ways to do the persuading when the workshop door slammed open to admit Connor Morrissey, agitated and out of breath.

"They're back," Connor said. "The cops. Liam says to shut down the workshop, and for the Goddess's sake, hide Jace."

Another thing Shifters could do, if Fionn was so interested, was galvanize themselves to move swiftly when need be. Dylan and Sean slid Collars and tools into hiding places with the smoothness of long practice, quickly placing the half-finished woodworking projects on the tables, scattering about tools and used sandpaper as though a woodworker had absently thrown them down.

Sean and Andrea departed without much of a goodbye, heading to wherever they'd prefer to be found. Deni helped Jace up from the floor, her touch the only thing keeping him from rushing out the door to confront the cops and keep them away from her.

"Where are they, Connor?" Deni was asking. "I need to get Jace back to my house."

Connor shook his head. "No time. Too many cops between here and there."

"I can hide the Shifter," Fionn said. He was the

calmest of all, as though the situation was one more interesting tidbit in his observation of humans and Shifters. "I don't want humans to find me either."

"Hide me how?" Jace asked, every nerve a line of fire. "I don't trust Fae."

"Very wise of you," Fionn said. "Fae are treacherous bastards, every single one of us. I should know. Come with me now, or end up in a cage to be poked at by humans. Your choice."

"Go." Deni kissed his cheek. "Dylan will take care of me."

Dylan, the powerful alpha Feline who liked to hug Deni. Jace would rather cave in Dylan's face and pull Deni with him to wherever the Fae was taking him. But putting Deni under the Fae's power wasn't what he wanted either. Jace hugged his arms over his chest, his instincts tearing through him, warring with his common sense. It was hell going feral.

"*Now*," Fionn said. He didn't touch Jace, as though he knew Jace would attack him if he did, but his voice impelled. Jace could well believe this man was a general.

Jace caught Deni around the waist. Her gray eyes were large, filled with fear, but behind the fear, Jace saw her mating frenzy answering his. He kissed her, savoring the taste of her warm lips, then he cupped her cheek, pulled on his jacket again, and followed Fionn into the night.

———

"AND YOU ARE?" THE FEMALE POLICE OFFICER ASKED Deni. The woman wore a bulletproof vest and a riot helmet and carried two pistols, while her male counterpart had a pistol and a tranq rifle.

They'd come prepared to do battle against Shifters if need be. They found most Shifters peacefully cooking out, as Sean was doing behind Liam's house.

"Deni Rowe." Deni handed the female cop her ID card, which each Shifter had to update every year. "Same as last time," she couldn't help adding. Both these officers had been in the group that had come to Deni's and Ellison's house.

"Hmm." The female officer peered at Deni's ID, shining a black light on it, pretending she wasn't nervous.

Dylan stood behind Deni, not wanting her to face the cops alone. Dylan said nothing and didn't try to interfere, but Dylan could unnerve most humans—not to mention most Shifters—simply by standing there. Both the male and female officer were sweating under his scrutiny.

"Seems okay." The female officer handed the card back to Deni. "Nice bracelet," she said, glancing at the gold chain on Deni's wrist.

"It was my mother's," Deni said. She tucked the ID into the back pocket of her shorts.

"Looks expensive." Shifters weren't allowed to wear costly jewelry, and shouldn't be able to afford to buy it.

"Handed down through the family," Deni answered. "I have photos of my mother and my grandmother wearing it, if you want to see them."

"Hmm." Another skeptical sound. "Where's the other guy? The one I saw you with before?"

Deni prayed these two weren't good at reading body

language as she answered nonchalantly, "Ellison? He's my brother. He's at the bar with his mate."

"I mean the other one. The drunk one you were with at the ... ceremony."

Damn it. "I don't know," Deni said. She took a step back to Dylan, putting herself into the radius of his warmth. "I'm with Dylan tonight."

Deni smiled at the female cop, as though willing her to understand. If humans liked to believe Shifter women were promiscuous, Deni would use it to her advantage. The female officer's look turned to disgust, but Deni didn't care what this woman thought of her as long as Jace was safe.

Both cops looked Dylan and Deni over and exchanged knowing smirks. They'd seen Dylan with Glory at the fight club. They must think Shiftertown was one big sex fest.

Dylan put his arm around Deni and dared them to say anything. The cops all but snickered as they moved off toward another set of Shifters walking on the dark street.

"Sorry," Deni said in a low voice to Dylan.

Dylan squeezed her shoulder. "You're good at thinking on your feet. Nothing to be sorry about." Another squeeze of reassurance, then he let her go. "But let's don't mention this to Glory."

Deni smiled. "No fear."

"She would understand eventually, but it's the 'eventually' that would be uncomfortable." Dylan sent her one of his rare smiles. "Let's go have some barbeque."

They had to, to keep up the verisimilitude. Deni only hoped Jace was safe, and that the half-crazed wolf inside her wouldn't make her break away from Dylan and race around Shiftertown until she could find and protect him again.

———

"So this is Faerie?" Jace wrinkled his nose at the smell. "I don't like it."

"As my daughter would say... Suck it up."

Shifters had left Faerie forever seven hundred years ago, not that they'd ever embraced it as home. Though they'd been created here, Shifters had cultivated a healthy loathing of the place.

Jace had followed Fionn to a grove of trees between the backyards of Shifter houses. In the glow of the few streetlights, he'd seen police officers walking from house to house, and patrol cars and vans creeping along the streets.

The darkness in the grove of trees had been deep, inky. A mist rose from nowhere in the middle of the ring of trees, one that smelled acrid to Jace. A tingling had begun in Jace's brain that had him snarling, his claws coming out, before Fionn had grabbed him and shoved him into the middle of the mist.

Jace had blinked, the tingling dying, and found himself in another ring of trees, these old, towering, and damp. His boots squished in mud covered with gray green weeds and dead leaves. The thick trees ran as far as Jace could see, the land wet, dank, and muddy.

"Boring," Jace said. "No wonder my ancestors chose to live in the human world."

Fionn made an impatient noise. "This is only one tiny corner of one woods in Faerie. I live miles from here in a valley that would put anything found in your world to shame. Mountains reaching to the skies, snowcaps burnished by the sun, meadows of grass so green it makes you weep, and packed with wildflowers in every color. My garden is designed to run right into the meadows, so it's as though I step into paradise every time I walk out my door. My manor house has marble floors, and walls veined with Fae gold, which humans have never seen—and never will. Fae gold is rare even for the Fae. Humans would kill each other—and Fae—over it."

"Walls veined with gold," Jace said. "No overkill there."

Fionn started walking into the trees, ignoring him. "When I come to this area, however, I live rough in a tent. This way."

"Wait a minute." Jace jogged to catch up with him. The Fae-man was *fast*. "How do you know where the gateway, or whatever that was, is? All these trees look alike— and smell alike—to me."

Fionn didn't look back. "Then you'd better stick with me, hadn't you?"

Great. "How do I know you're not leading me to Fae warriors with big swords who'd love a Shifter snow leopard head decorating their fireplace?"

"You don't," Fionn said. "You have to trust me."

"Thanks. I feel so much better."

It was then that Jace noticed he *did* feel better. The feral restlessness had eased from him, the pain of his Collar lessening. When he put his hand to his neck, he still felt the soreness—did he ever—but the certainty he'd drop dead any second had gone.

Fionn led him around three gigantic trees growing close together and stopped in front of a pavilion. *Tent,* Fionn had called it. *Ballroom-sized living space,* Jace would term it instead.

He followed Fionn inside, though his Shifter instincts did not want him to. The interior of the pavilion was as lavish as the exterior. It had been divided into rooms by tapestries hung from solid rods, and carpeted with rugs that looked as though they were made of woven silk. Low couches, chairs, and tables were scattered everywhere, and a large brazier burned with a fire that cut the damp.

"You call *this* living rough?" Jace asked, turning in a circle. Everywhere he saw light, color, and shimmering texture.

"You've been living in human rejects too long. This is what you could have in Faerie, and much better than this."

"Not as a Shifter slave I couldn't," Jace pointed out.

"Possibly not. Though I don't keep slaves. Any Shifters who lived in my realm would be free to come and go as they pleased."

A fair-minded Fae? "Good to know," Jace said.

"I can't speak for other Fae, though," Fionn said. "So if you went outside my territory, yes, you'd probably end up a slave or a mantelpiece decoration."

"You're so comforting."

"Wine?" Fionn poured a golden, smoothly trickling liquid into a cup. "Best I can get out here. The good stuff doesn't transport well."

Never drink anything offered by a Fae. The old tales about Fae, passed down by Shifters, rang in Jace's head. His dad used to tell him the stories, as had Aunt Cass. Jace said nothing, but couldn't stop himself from taking a step back.

Fionn laughed. "You're superstitious. But probably wise. I know Fae who try to drug, poison, or spell everyone they meet. You're lucky I'm not interested. If I want someone under my thrall, I'll take over their territory and let them choose between following me or being put to the sword."

"What a nice guy," Jace said dryly. Fionn held out the cup, but Jace shook his head. Even if Fionn proved to be trustworthy, Jace couldn't be certain what Fae wine would do to his system, especially as traumatized as it had been lately. Fionn shrugged, lifted the wine cup to his lips, and drained its contents.

Jace looked around the lush living quarters, again reflecting that he felt much better. He was afraid to pursue why. If living in Faerie was the only way to stop Shifters who had their Collars removed from going feral, he'd rather take his chances being feral.

"So tell me," Jace said, as Fionn poured himself more wine. "If this is more or less the armpit of Faerie, why do you come out here?"

Fionn lowered his cup. When he spoke, his voice was softer. "To be near my daughter."

"Oh."

Fionn raised his brows and drank deeply again. "Yes, I am that maudlin. But I had to give up Andrea for more than forty years. I want to spend as much time with her as I possibly can. And my grandson."

"I get that."

The hard-faced warrior suddenly looked much older

and more vulnerable. "That's why I conquered this part of Faerie. So I could see her without anyone being the wiser. I'm alone now, but Andrea makes life worth living."

"You old softie," Jace said, grinning.

"I am. I admit it without shame. Make yourself comfortable, Shifter. This might take some time. Dylan will send word when the way is safe."

———

Deni didn't want to eat, but she managed to choke down a burger Sean prepared for her, made with sautéed mushrooms and Havarti cheese, which Deni loved. Mouthwatering goodness, but tonight, Deni had no appetite.

The police still roamed Shiftertown. They'd interrogated the Shifters in Liam's yard—including Deni, again—and now they wandered the blocks.

Deni noticed that they'd left the cubs who'd gathered at Liam's alone. A large number of cubs had found their way here, sent by their parents for safety, and now they sat on the porch and its steps, devouring Sean's burgers. Spike's cub, Jordan, Olaf the polar bear, the older bear girl named Cherie Liam and Kim's little girl on Kim's lap, and others from around the town. Andrea carried her son and helped Kim look after the kids, but mostly the cubs had been sent here because of Tiger.

The police hadn't talked to Tiger much, leaving him and Tiger's mate, Carly, pretty much alone. They hadn't gone near the cubs at all, because Tiger had positioned himself between the police officers and the cubs on the porch. The officers, after taking one look at Tiger, had seemed to tacitly agree to stop even looking at the kids.

The cops might have the badges, armor, guns, and authority, Deni reflected, but in this corner of Shiftertown, Tiger had the power. The police seemed to know it, just as small animals knew they were prey for the cat that strolled by, even if the cat wasn't attacking. They'd feel better once the cat was gone, and they could duck inside their holes again for safety.

Even after the police finally left the yard, Tiger remained on guard. The huge man with black and orange hair unnerved even the Shifters. The only adult truly comfortable with him was Carly, a young woman with honey brown hair who wrapped her hands around Tiger's big arm and smiled up at him. She was just beginning to show her pregnancy, and the look Tiger gave her warmed Deni's heart.

Those two had found love. Knowing what Tiger and Carly had gone through, Deni felt a lick of hope that she too could find happiness—even with the Feline Shifter who was right now hiding out in Faerie, and who couldn't legally be in her Shiftertown.

"He'll have to go," Dylan said to Sean not two feet away from Deni.

Deni turned to them, not bothering to pretend not to listen. If they hadn't wanted her to hear, Dylan wouldn't have said anything while she was standing so close.

Sean, turning burgers with tongs, nodded. "We'll have to try again later."

They were going to send Jace home, while he was half-crazed with the partially removed Collar, and wait for who knew how long. She opened her mouth to argue, but Dylan shook his head.

"You know I'm right, Den," Dylan said. "We can't risk that the cops won't start taking roll call in all Shiftertowns. I'll get him home as soon as I'm able."

Deni nodded. True, Jace would be safer at his own Shiftertown, where he had his father and family to take care of him. But Deni's heart felt like a stone in her chest, and her food tasted like dust.

She set the plate down, nodded at Sean and Dylan, and walked in a daze toward the porch and the cubs. Deni wished Ellison and her sons were here—she needed to wrap herself in her family to ease the sudden pain.

Andrea seemed to sense her need. She handed her little boy to Kim and met Deni in the yard, pulling her into a hug.

"I know," Andrea said. "I saw it in your eyes when you looked at him tonight. Don't worry. I'll tell Liam, and we'll make it so you can see him again."

Andrea was sweet; she truly was. Andrea herself had been given special permission to move from a Colorado Shiftertown to this one, which proved it could be done, but she'd had to jump through many hoops to do it. Deni knew she could see Jace again, but it would be tough, and both Liam and Jace's father would have to be convinced that it was necessary for either Jace or Deni to move permanently.

Andrea released Deni, giving her a reassuring smile, and returned to the porch to lift her cub from Kim's lap. The look of joy she turned on her son squeezed Deni's heart.

"Don't let him go."

Deni jumped and swung around, her wolf's senses sending her into a defensive crouch. Tiger had moved to her side in that stealthy way he had, and now he stood right next to her, alone, his bulk filling the space Andrea had vacated.

"Tiger." Deni straightened up and clenched her hands. "Don't *do* that."

"You should not let Jace go home," Tiger said. "Keep him with you."

"I can't," Deni said. "He doesn't belong here, and if they catch him ..."

Tiger shook his head. He reached out his hand, carefully, and touched the air in front of Deni's chest, as though he saw something there. Deni felt the warmth inside her, the tingling need she'd been pretending not to notice.

"You have it, don't you?" Tiger said. "Don't let it go."

Deni swallowed. If she admitted the mate bond right now, she'd fall in a crumpled heap and begin weeping. "I—"

"Tiger, honey," Carly strolled to him and laced her hands around his arm again. "Don't scare her. She's been through a lot."

Tiger only looked at Deni with his intense yellow eyes, as though willing her to understand and obey. He let Carly lead him away, but he glanced at Deni over his shoulder, his gaze penetrating to the most frightened part of her.

When Jace emerged from Faerie into the grove of trees in Shiftertown, it was dawn. Shiftertown was quiet, the nocturnal Shifters having turned in to sleep, the ones who lived by human schedules not up yet.

Dylan met him. Dylan's face was covered with new-growth beard, and lines had deepened about his eyes. He hadn't slept all night.

Time moved differently in Faerie, Fionn had told Jace, sometimes slower, sometimes faster. Jace had spent twice as many hours there as the time had moved here.

Scary. What if he popped into Faerie one day, lived a week, and came out to find everyone long dead? Or he aged in Faerie while Deni had lived only one day? Too weird to contemplate. The solution was not to go to Faerie again, which was fine with Jace.

He still felt better, even with the Collar's loose links chafing him. He'd have to figure out why he seemed to have recovered from his need to go feral, and if whatever he discovered could help with removing the Collars.

The police had given up harassing the Shifters and gone again, Dylan said, but there was no telling when they'd be back. Best Jace go home, to his own Shiftertown. Jace couldn't argue with his reasoning, though leaving meant leaving Deni, and that thought threatened to make his feral rage return.

Fionn hadn't accompanied Jace. Dylan told Jace to wait for him there, while he arranged transportation to the airstrip. He walked away, leaving Jace alone.

Not for long. As soon as Dylan left the grove, Deni hurried into it.

Jace said nothing, only opened his arms, and Deni ran straight into them. Jace caught her up, turning around with her, holding her hard, breathing in her warmth, her scent.

———

"I DON'T WANT YOU TO GO," DENI SAID. SHE CURLED her hands against Jace's chest, where his heart was pounding.

"I don't want to go either."

Their mouths met, locking together, heat joining heat. Jace drank her hungrily, imbibing her spice. He licked the corner of her mouth, and moved one hand to her lush breast.

"Den," he said savagely, "I haven't... Finding you..."

Is all the world to me, Deni finished inside her head. *I was drowning, far from shore. And then you came.*

"Tiger told me not to let you go," she whispered.

Jace lifted his head, his green eyes dark. "I have to. If they find me, it will be bad for everyone here, not only me."

"I know. I know."

"I can't let you get hurt because of me." Jace traced her cheek with a firm thumb. "But I'll fix this. I'll find a way to come back as soon as I can."

Deni nodded, tears filling her eyes. No reason to cry, she told herself. This was smart, and he'd just promised to come back for her.

She heard Tiger's gruff voice in her head. *Don't let him go.*

Everyone knew Tiger was a little nuts, but he'd looked at Deni as though he could see the threads of the mate bond around her heart. He was telling her to latch on to the bond and not let go, damn the consequences.

But Deni needed to be sensible. If they did everything by the book, asking for official permission for Jace to move here, or she and her sons to go with him, then the humans couldn't legally keep them apart. But permission was difficult to obtain—the human government might deny it for any number of reasons, and then it would be more difficult for Jace or Deni to sneak away to be together.

"You could always hide here until they get tired of looking," Deni said, though without much hope.

Jace shook his head, pressing her closer. "Dylan's right. The police might start checking the other Shiftertowns. My dad can't cover for me for long."

"I know." His words made sense, but Deni's heart ached. She tried to smile. "The next time you come, we'll take my motorcycle out on one of the back roads and see what it can do. We'll open it up—just us and the wind."

"Yeah." Jace cupped her cheek. "That sounds good."

They kissed again, mouths seeking, needy, each of them holding on tight. Deni memorized Jace's scent and his goodness, his taste, his hard body against hers. He was large, strong, whole, the answer to her emptiness.

From beyond them, Dylan cleared his throat, the sound rolling from the edge of the grove. Jace broke the kiss, lifting slowly away from Deni. His green eyes held anguish. "I have to go."

"Wait." Deni fumbled with the catch of her bracelet, an old-fashioned clasp. The bracelet had been in her family for so long, no one remembered where it had come from. She took off the bracelet and pressed it into Jace's hand. "Keep this for me. Bring it back to me."

Jace started to shake his head. "It's special to you, I can tell."

"It is. But if I know you have it, that will be special too."

Jace hesitated another moment, then he closed his fingers around it. "I'll keep it safe. I promise."

Deni nodded. She stepped back from him and clasped her hands. "The Goddess go with you."

"No." Jace reached for her once more, his arms coming hard around her. "That's what you say to someone you'll never see again."

His kiss was fierce, wild. Deni held on to Jace and kissed him back with as much force, her heart pounding and aching.

At last Jace eased away, and Deni made herself let him go. Jace laid his hand on her chest, between her breasts.

"Be well, my heart," he said, then he turned and walked away, following Dylan into the Texas dawn.

———

There was no question of Deni coming with Jace to the plane. Jace understood—the fewer Shifters who left Shiftertown the better.

Jace hunkered down with a bunch of junk in the bed of Dylan's small pickup, and Dylan tied a tarp over it all. Then Dylan drove out of Shiftertown without ceremony, heading east along the Bastrop Highway.

After a long time, Dylan took a turn off the main road, pulled over, and lifted the tarp. The road was deserted, and Jace climbed out, stretching his cramped limbs. Dylan would leave Jace here to wait for a human man to come by who would take him the rest of the way to the airstrip— they'd done this on Jace's previous trips as well. Safer for all concerned if a Shifter wasn't spotted driving out to an abandoned airfield.

"Be well," Dylan said, clasping Jace in a brief but tight hug. "I'll work on things from here."

Jace nodded his thanks, jogged into the tall grasses, and crouched down, hiding himself, to wait. Dylan got back into his truck and drove smoothly away before any other vehicles came down the road.

Jace didn't wait long, though it felt like forever as he lay in the dew-laden grass. Another pickup, which was driven by one of the men he'd seen this trip at the landing strip, slowed down and waited for Jace to climb inside the cab.

Fifteen minutes and an unpaved road later, Jace was back at the airstrip, boarding the small, old cargo plane a man named Marlo flew. Marlo had long ago worked for very bad men, transporting things for them from Mexico, but had given it up. Now he smuggled Shifters anywhere in the country they wanted to go.

"Let's get up in the air," Marlo said, ushering Jace up the little stair into the body of the plane. "The wind is getting bad. Want to get out of this system."

To Jace, the sky was clear and beautiful, only a little breeze stirring the grasses around them. But pilots spoke a different language.

Jace stowed his backpack, then took the copilot's seat in the cockpit. He didn't know how to fly, but Marlo tended to talk a lot on the trips, and Jace always felt better if Marlo faced forward, looking at his instruments, than if he constantly turned around to yell at Jace in the back.

Marlo did his checks, started up, checked some more instruments, waved at the ground crew, and taxied out to the grown-over airstrip. The two men at the tiny shed waved back, then returned to the pickup that had brought Jace and drove away.

Marlo sped the plane down the little runway, bouncing over ruts, then lifted off without much of a bump. The plane flopped around a little as they climbed, buffeted by the winds Marlo had mentioned, but soon they were running in a fairly smooth layer of air.

The city of Austin spread out to the north of them, hugging the river and its hills, the river country receding to a streak of vivid green in the otherwise dry Texas brown.

Jace opened his hand and studied the bracelet resting

in his palm. Delicate, yet strong, like Deni was. He rubbed his thumb over the smooth gold, determined to see her smile at him when he brought it back to her.

He growled. Jace already missed her like crazy, and the wildcat in him snarled at him for walking away. The torn skin on his neck hurt again, the soreness making his beast that much angrier. Whatever mitigating effects being in Faerie had given him must be wearing off.

Interesting about that. Jace let the bracelet trickle over his hand as he thought. Maybe they should try taking off the Collars inside Faerie. Then again, what if inside Faerie Shifters behaved normally and then went insane when they walked out once more?

Jace let out a sigh. He'd been full of enthusiasm about removing the Collars when he'd come to Austin, but things had changed. He no longer wanted to risk himself for what might be. He had something to lose now. If the Morrisseys wanted to experiment with the Collars so much, they could, as Fionn might say, suck it up, and test it on themselves.

His gaze returned to the bracelet, and he imagined it still warm from Deni's wrist ...

The plane bounced once, hard, as though it had hit some kind of airborne speed bump. Marlo shouted, "Whoa!" and grabbed for the stick as dials started spinning.

"Whoa *what?*" Jace yelled over the engines that had started to roar. "You can fix that, right?"

"Shit," Marlo said. He added quickly, "Nothing to worry about—this has happened before. I need to set down. Help me look for a place."

"Nothing to worry about?" The plane was heading downward, leaving Jace's stomach behind, everything in back banging and clattering. Another bump shook the plane, which nosed harder downward.

The small airplane gave a profound rattle and smoke poured out the left-side engine, flames licking the wing.

"The engine's on fire!" Jace shouted. "You call that nothing to worry about?"

"The wind will put it out. Help me look!"

"Aw, crap on a crutch," Jace snarled.

He wrapped his hand around the bracelet and held it hard, as though it were a link to Deni herself.

Goddess, Goddess, great and good, Jace began the ritual prayer, then gave up trying to remember the words. *Help me. Let me be with Deni again. I feel the mate bond, for crying out loud.*

The warmth in his heart he'd told himself he didn't yet have time to think about, now suffused his body.

Saying good-bye to Deni had been one of the hardest things Jace had ever done. Jace had been ripping out his heart and walking away bleeding, but he'd made himself do it, believing leaving was the right thing to do.

The mate bond meant you gave yourself to that other person, body and soul. You protected them, they healed you, and you healed them while they protected you.

Jace didn't know if Deni felt the mate bond for him—sometimes both parties didn't share it—but he remembered the look in her gray eyes before he'd left her.

She had to feel it. They'd grown from acquaintances to lovers to mates rapidly, but it often happened like that with

Shifters. Shifters formed the mate bond, *then* they got to know each other—throughout their long, happy lives.

And now, with Marlo fighting this tiny bird, fire whipping around the wing, and the flat ground of West Texas coming up fast, Jace might never move beyond knowing the mate bond had settled in his heart.

Tiger told me not to let you go.

Tiger, damn his crazy, striped ass, had been right. He might not have predicted *this*, specifically, but he'd known Jace should have made sure he stayed next to Deni and figured things out from there.

Something cut his palm. Jace opened his hand and saw he'd clutched the gold bracelet so hard it had pressed into his skin.

Jace clenched the bracelet again and shook his fist at Marlo, the ends of the chains dancing. "Fix this damned thing. I'm taking this back to her."

"You are fucking crazy, Shifter. I need a landing strip, or I'm not fixing anything ever again."

"Shit," Jace said. He'd been scanning the ground, but what did he know about good places to put down a plane? Then he saw it, a flat stretch of land, unbroken, a dirt road without an oil well at the end of it. They were low enough now that he could see the way wasn't full of rocks or hidden washes. "What about that?"

"Good enough for me."

The plane was rattling with bone-jarring intensity, something popping in the back like a row of fireworks. Jace prayed it wasn't really fireworks.

The road came at them, Marlo desperately pulling at

the stick to lift the nose enough. The wheels were down, at least, because Marlo had never pulled them up.

"Hang on!" Marlo yelled.

To what? Jace braced himself on the instrument panel, trying not to look at the dials going around and around.

They hit the road with an upward burst of dust, grinding it so thick it coated the windows, blocking their visibility. That was fine, because grass and whatever huge weeds this part of the state grew came up out of the ground and bashed into them, winding around the burning engine and spewing the flame higher.

The plane hit something and skidded sideways, throwing Marlo on top of Jace, and whipping Jace into the window. The window cracked, and flame raced inside.

At the last minute, Jace yanked off his seat belt, hauled himself out of the chair, threw the already unconscious Marlo to the bottom of the plane, and landed on top of him. A roar of explosion met Jace's ears, and then nothing.

CHAPTER ELEVEN

Deni was restless all morning. She tried to work in the yard, neatening her garden, but she found herself stabbing the trowel into the dirt again and again for no reason. Deni threw down the trowel and stripped off her gloves, dropping them as well.

Her arm felt bare and strange without the bracelet she wore all the time. She touched her skin there but smiled. The bracelet was safe with Jace. He'd come back to her.

Still, she was growling by the time she reached the house. Jackson hadn't been scheduled to work today, but Will now gave Deni a good-bye hug and went off to the warehouse.

"You all right, Mom?" Jackson said, peering at Deni after they waved off Will.

Jackson looked so much like his father, his hair dark instead of light like hers and Ellison's, his eyes a lighter shade of gray. Deni pulled him into a hug, feeling a flood of love for him.

She remembered when her mate had been dying, how the mate bond had pulled at her and sickened her . . . as it was doing now.

A reaction to Jace leaving so abruptly, she told herself. *Nothing is wrong.*

"I'm fine," she said.

"It's just that you look at little bit, you know." Jackson frowned in worry. "Like you do when you start to go feral."

He trailed off, and nausea bit Deni, the world spinning. She gripped Jackson's shoulder. "No, don't let me—" *Forget who everyone is, try to attack my own children. Goddess, please!*

She smelled a strong, male smell, one different enough from other Shifters to make her wolf's hackles rise. Deni growled and spun around, instinctively stepping in front of Jackson, protecting.

Tiger stood at the edge of the yard, having suddenly appeared as he usually did. Deni took a deep breath, willing herself to calm.

"You let him go," Tiger said.

Deni shook her head, the nausea still churning. "I didn't have a choice."

He waited until she came to him, not violating Ellison's territory. Deni felt herself drawn to him, though, as though she needed to go to him. Unnerving.

Tiger let his hand hover a few inches from her chest, as he'd done last night. "Something is wrong."

Fear washed cold through her. "How do you know?"

"The mate bond." Tiger closed his fingers over empty air. "It's telling you."

The logical Deni wanted to argue, to deny. The feral beast inside Deni knew. Jace was in danger.

Tiger pinned her with his yellow stare, then turned around and walked away. Deni's heart beat faster, and she almost snarled when she felt Jackson's warmth suddenly behind her.

She blinked, Jackson's worried face coming back into focus.

"I'm all right," she said to him, drawing a deep breath. "I need to make a phone call."

She hurried into the house, found her cell phone, and rushed across the street after Tiger to ask for the phone number of Eric Warden and his son, Jace.

———

THE SNOW LEOPARD CHOKED ON THE BLACK SMOKE, paws scrabbling at the hole in the fuselage to find air, any air. He burned himself on the hot metal and snarled, but he needed to get his nose out of the plane and breathe.

More scrambling, using Shifter wildcat strength and huge claws to tear into the metal. His cat brain reflected that having someone like Ronan the Kodiak bear around would be very useful right now, then he went back to the task at hand. Human thought fled, and animal ones took over.

Hole wider. Heave from back legs, wriggle spine, pull with shoulders, scramble *out*. Jace landed on top of the wreckage—on the side of the plane that had tipped over—and tried to take a deep breath. Too much smoke. He had to get away.

The engine was burning merrily, and Jace's cat nose smelled fuel. He needed to run, *now*.

A groan made him turn back, his claws raking against metal. A human lay in the wreckage, a lean man with a scraggly beard who was a little bit smelly. *Marlo*, his brain reminded him.

Jace was Shifter. He didn't need a human slowing him down and returning him to captivity. Now was his chance to run, to be free, to find a place where humans would never hunt him down. He'd get word to his mate somehow, she'd come to him, and they'd live in blissful solitude forever.

Another groan. Jace's ears went flat on his head, his cat instincts telling him to run and not stop. But he turned and lowered his body back into the wreck.

He found Marlo trapped under a pile of metal and junk, barely alive. Jace shoved at the debris, trying to reach him. Something in Jace's brain told him to shift back to human so he could lift Marlo, but his body wouldn't obey. Being animal was the best way to survive, so animal he stayed.

Fire flared high, and the temperature in the wreck doubled. The smoke thickened. Jace couldn't breathe, couldn't cough, could no longer see. He put his mouth around the back of Marlo's neck and heaved.

The trouble with humans was they had no scruff. If Jace bit down too hard, he'd sever the man's spine and kill him. Not enough, and he wouldn't be able to carry him.

Jace finally got a decent hold on Marlo's neck and shirt, and dragged him out from under the debris. With the last breath in his lungs, Jace clawed his way up through the hole again, weighted down by the extra body. He dropped Marlo on top of the plane, seeing that he'd cut gashes into the man's neck.

Out here Jace could get his breath, but it was still tainted with the heavy smoke. Marlo lay unmoving, and Jace couldn't tell whether he was breathing.

He got his jaws around the man's shirt and neck again and scrambled off the wreckage to the ground. Once he felt the dirt under his feet, he ran, loping almost sideways as he dragged Marlo with him. Marlo's feet bump-bumped over the dry grasses.

When they were about fifty feet from the plane, the fire caught the fuel's fumes and exploded. Fire washed over Jace, who threw himself on top of Marlo. Jace smelled his fur burning and drew in a lungful of volcanic air. Burning metal rained around them, sparking on the dry grass, which obligingly caught fire.

Jace hauled himself up, knowing he was on fire, and dragged Marlo down into the sparse rocks that lined a shallow wash. The wash was dry, no water under the blank blue sky, but it might protect them from the flames.

Jace dropped Marlo and rolled over the rocks, writhing desperately to grind out the fire in his fur. Marlo lay unmoving, bloody and burned, but he didn't smell dead.

Now that he wasn't burning alive and could breathe, Jace noticed all the hurts in his body, cuts from crawling out of the plane, abrasions and rawness from shielding Marlo. His left paw hurt like hell, a stinging pain that meant he'd cut himself deeply.

Jace rose stiffly from his crouch in the wash and looked around. The plane burned by itself in the middle of nothing. West Texas sprawled around them, empty as far as Jace's leopard eyes could see. Someone likely owned this land, maybe it was part of a gigantic ranch, but out here, entire counties might have only a handful of houses in them.

Jace shook himself, aching all over, but he considered himself lucky. He hadn't broken anything as far as he could tell, and though chunks of his fur had burned off and his skin smarted, he would heal.

His left paw hurt like hell, though. The last thing he remembered was clutching Deni's bracelet as the plane hit the earth. Jace flexed the pads of his empty paw and looked back at the burning wreck. He'd dropped the bracelet. Deni's bracelet, which he'd promised to keep safe for her. *No.*

He started to run back toward the plane before his leopard brain stopped him. *Let it go.* The mate bond wrapping him whimpered. That bracelet had been part of her, and she'd entrusted it to him.

Let it go. Think. Survive.

Flee.

Jace was free. No one knew where he was. When humans came to find the plane, they wouldn't even know he'd been in it. He'd been smuggled goods. Shifters, including Deni and his family, would think him dead inside it. Deni would cry. So would his dad.

Grief bit at Jace, but in his cat form, survival came first. He scanned the ground again. The first thing he noticed was a coyote, thin-legged and mangy, waiting to see if the two from the wreck would die. Easier pickings than rabbits the coyote had to chase.

Dark specks appeared in the sky as well, circling higher as they spotted Jace looking at them. Turkey buzzards, big and black, they also waiting to see whether they'd feast today. This was the kill-or-be-killed wild out here, no rules in sight.

Jace snarled and rushed at the coyote. The flea-bitten beast snarled in response but fled. Not far, though. Out of reach of Jace's charge, the coyote stopped and waited.

Jace growled his challenge. In spite of being half-burned and thrown around a wreck, Jace felt strong, more so than he had in a long time. The pain of his Collar was completely gone, and in fact, he couldn't even feel the Collar biting into him anymore. He shook himself again and sat down to let his back paw reach up to his neck to scratch.

He stopped. His delicate back toes didn't find a chain, burned or loose, or tight and whole. He swiped his neck with a front paw, with the same result.

Jace told himself to shift, to make sure, and he would—when he could remember how to. The leopard wanted to stay in this form, so Jace was staying in this form.

He writhed around, trying to find the Collar with each of his paws in turn, probably to the amusement of the coyote. Actually, the coyote didn't care—he was simply waiting to see whether Jace would be food or danger.

No, wait—the coyote had vanished. Damn him, he'd been sneaking up on Marlo while Jace went through his contortions. The coyote darted in, ready to drag Marlo—or pieces of him—away to his pack.

Jace went for the coyote. Ears up, paws moving in

perfect rhythm, Jace rushed the scavenger. He didn't snarl or make any noise—he didn't have to.

The coyote barely got away from Jace's striking paw. Jace caught his tail with a claw, causing the coyote to yelp and run. Jace chased him, the leopard rejoicing in the hunt, until he realized that the buzzards had taken the opportunity to land near Marlo and see if there were any good pickings.

Jace turned and barreled toward the birds, who flapped away with slow disdain. He snarled this time, making his fur stand up so he'd be large and menacing.

He knew for certain that his Collar was gone when he finally stopped and planted himself near Marlo. He'd been ready to kill the coyote and savage its body, and the Collar hadn't tried to stop him. Jace had mastered the meditation technique, yes, but out here, chasing away scavengers while trying to stay away from a burning plane, he hadn't exactly been meditating.

The Collar was gone. Completely. It must have fallen off in the wreckage or while Jace had been dragging Marlo away from it.

That meant that somehow in the burning mess that had been Marlo's airplane, Jace's Collar had slipped off, every link of it, without hurting him and without making the world spin into insanity.

Jace sat, blinking, even his leopard realizing the enormity of it. Now, if he could shift back to human, find his way home, and try to figure out exactly how it had happened, all Shifters would benefit.

Or he could stay in the wild. For the first time in twenty years, Jace was *free*. No more Collar, no more rules, no Shiftertowns, just wind, earth, sky, and small-brained predators.

Free, he repeated.

The only thing that kept his triumphant wildcat from taking over and erasing his human thoughts completely was one word.

Deni.

Jace would find her and free her too. Then he'd live out his life with her, the mate of his heart. No one in this wide wilderness would be able to prevail against a wolf and a snow leopard. He and Deni would be free to be alone together, mates in the wild, as Shifters were meant to be.

Even in this vast place, someone would have reported a crashing plane by now. The humans would be coming. Jace didn't intend to let them find him here.

He grabbed Marlo by the shirt, dragged him closer to the burning wreckage, which would keep the scavengers away for a while, then turned and loped off into the tall Texas grasses. His paw still hurt him, but that was a minor inconvenience.

————

ERIC HADN'T HEARD FROM HIS SON ALL DAY, HE TOLD Deni, and Jace likely had his cell phone off. Eric was worried too, but Marlo's plane was old and slow. It wouldn't land in Las Vegas until late in the evening, but Eric would keep his ear out. He sounded plenty anxious but tried to calm Deni's fears, as a good Shifter leader should.

Liam too reassured her. Flying under the radar took

time, Marlo often stopped to refuel or lie low for a few hours. Marlo had a cell phone, but he wasn't answering either, and he didn't always.

After Liam left to open the bar in the afternoon, Deni paced, snapped at everyone, and got nothing done. Any pats on the back or calming words only irritated her.

Eric and Liam were probably right—but Tiger's words about seeing something wrong with the mate bond, plus the tightness in Deni's chest made her half crazy.

Ellison left for the bar not long behind Liam, telling Deni and his mate that Liam had called a tracker meeting. That meant trackers only—the Shifters who worked for Liam as bodyguards, investigators, or peacekeepers as need be.

Ronan, Ellison, Spike, Sean, Tiger, and Dylan made their way there, leaving Deni restless and barely in control of herself.

At five, she couldn't stand it anymore. Deni walked out of the house and down the block, making her way to the bar on the edge of Shiftertown.

The parking lot was already full. This bar was a popular stop on the way home from work for humans who liked Shifters. Groupies were already there, lounging about suggestively, waiting for Shifters to come looking. With the fight club shut down for a while, the groupies had decided to pile on here, it seemed.

The human bartender shot Deni a sharp look when she walked in. The other Shifters already there were cagey, but when Deni asked why, they didn't have an answer. They knew something was up, but they didn't know what.

The trackers had gone into Liam's office and shut the

door, they told her, then all except Liam and Dylan had come out and left the bar. Where the trackers, including Ellison, had gone, no one knew.

Deni had no business confronting Liam, who wasn't in her pack and held plenty of rank over her. His tracker meeting might have nothing to do with her or Jace, or the police. Shit involving Shifters and Shiftertown happened all the time.

One of the groupie girls sat in a booth by herself, talking on her phone. And talking and talking. She'd look around, and then start talking again. If she wasn't talking, she was texting.

The young woman didn't look much different from the other groupies. She wore a short, skintight pink dress with mile-high black heels, had short dyed-black hair that had been cut into cute wisps, and she'd painted her face with cat's eyes and whiskers. Her outfit shouted, *Come and get me, Shifter, I like to purr,* but her looks and actions spoke of extreme nerves.

After Deni had watched her covertly for a time, she realized another thing that made this woman different. The other groupies were eyeing Shifters hungrily, or sashaying up to them without shame. Most groupies were female, as many of the Shifters here were male, but some young male groupies were eyeing the male Shifters—and Deni—with the same kind of interest.

The young woman in the booth was doing her best *not* to catch any Shifter's attention. Which made no sense if she dressed like a groupie and hung out in a Shifter bar.

Deni picked up the bottle of beer the bartender had slid to her and carried it with her to the booth. Deni plunked the bottle onto the table and sat down opposite the young woman.

The young woman jumped as though struck by sparks. Deni held her gaze, the girl trying to evade her eyes.

"That Shifter over there." Deni pointed. "Broderick. He's looking for some action."

Whether Broderick was or not, Deni didn't know, but the young woman's reaction was telling. She flinched and didn't look where Deni indicated. In fact, she moved a little so Deni would block Broderick's line of sight from her.

"I'm waiting for someone," the young woman mumbled. "Leave me alone, Shifter."

"Yeah? Who are you waiting for?"

The woman stared at her. She had light blue eyes and smelled strongly of fear, and even more of anger.

"None of your business." She had defiance her words and eyes, but her voice shook.

"Interesting," Deni said. She snatched the woman's cell phone from her hand and stood up.

The girl shrieked. "Hey, give that back!"

Deni stepped away from her reaching hands and scrolled down her list of recent calls. Only one had been made today, much earlier this afternoon, which meant she'd been faking talking to someone. Stalling.

She'd made plenty of calls yesterday, though, and the day before that, and on into the previous week. All to the City of Austin police.

"Don't think so," Deni said.

Broderick turned around, scowling, not liking to have

his beer drinking with his brothers interrupted. "Who the hell is making all the noise?" Broderick growled.

Deni ignored him. She swung away from the groupie lunging for her phone and went for Liam's office door. This was too important for respecting Liam's privacy.

"Broderick, don't let her leave," Deni said, then was through the door and into the office.

Liam was on the phone at his desk, Dylan hovering next to him, listening. Usually Liam sat back here with his feet up, casually going over billing, invoices, payroll, and the like, but today he sat straight up in his chair, his hand over his eyes, and he was speaking rapidly into the phone.

"Have you pinpointed where?" he asked whoever was on the other end. "Well, damn it, *find* it."

"Find what?" Cold washed through Deni, triggering the dizziness she'd been fighting all day. "Liam?"

Dylan came quickly around Deni and closed the door. "Keep it down, lass. We can't let the world know."

"Know what? Damn it, *tell me.*"

Liam glanced up at her, his face strained as he listened to the stream of words coming from his phone. He shot a look at his father and nodded.

Dylan took Deni's hand between his, pressing warmth into it.

"We didn't want you to know until we were sure, Den. Marlo's plane went down, somewhere in West Texas. We don't know where yet, and we don't know who survived."

CHAPTER TWELVE

Deni's world stopped—or maybe it kept spinning, whirling out of control while she froze in one place. She could barely see Dylan as she stared at him, only the blue of his eyes as he held her gaze.

Shock and then panic swept through her, and her wolf started to howl, a grief-stricken, wild howl that only happened with the death of a mate.

"Deni," Dylan's voice cut through the noise. "Keep looking at me."

The voice that came out of Deni's mouth was snarling and wrong. "Where is he?"

"South of I-10," Liam said. "Somewhere between here and Fort Stockton. Great," he said into the phone. "Covers a hell of a lot of ground."

Deni heard a voice on the other end—Ronan, she thought, from the deep timbre. "That's all we know," Ronan said. "We can't ask too many questions."

"Ask," Deni snarled. "Find him."

"Lass," Dylan said.

"Don't 'lass' me. Find him. He's my *mate*."

Both Dylan and Liam focused on her, as the truth of it filled Deni, hurting her and elating her at the same time.

My mate. Hurt. Lost. Find!

Deni was growling again, the edges of her world going concave as her eyes changed to her wolf's. Dylan pried the cell phone she'd taken from the girl out of her hand, which Deni had clamped down on so hard the plastic was starting to crack.

"Where did you get this?" Dylan asked, looking at the smart phone, which no Shifter would carry.

"Spy," Deni said, forcing out the word. "Broderick has."

Dylan's eyes moved as he read the phone numbers, then he gave a furious snarl and shoved his way past Deni, banging out of the office.

Deni yanked Liam's phone from his hands. "Ronan. You tell me where he is."

"Deni?" Ronan's tone softened. "Yeah, thought so. Sean's hacking as fast as he can. He's trying to pin down the location based on reports."

"Where are you?"

"Don't know." Ronan turned away from the phone, exchanging questions with others. "Looks like we're about where the 55 runs into the 277, wherever that is. A little west of that. Ellison says don't you dare come out here."

"Tell Ellison ..."

Deni's coherence left her. She didn't remember dropping the phone or saying anything to Liam. She only knew she was walking out through the bar, past Dylan, who had the pseudo-groupie pinned between himself and Broderick, ignoring them when they tried to stop her.

She walked and walked until she found herself in front of her own house, pulling out the new motorcycle Ellison had bought her and mounting it.

Deni must have found the keys, put on her helmet, jeans, and boots. She didn't remember. In a few minutes, she was pulling out of Shiftertown, skimming through traffic to the roads that led west out of town.

Deni didn't know Texas like Ellison did, but she knew how to get from Austin across the Hill Country west, heading through Fredericksburg toward the 10. At the onramp to the interstate, she paused, debating whether to go north or south. She picked north, turning again after about thirty miles to the 377 and cutting south.

Not until she was well down the highway, heading south and west as fast as she could, did she realize she was riding her motorcycle.

Alone. Out on the road, under the sky, through the flat Texas lands and dust. On her own. No one with her, no Jace holding her and telling her she could do it.

She'd navigated traffic that moved thickly to Fredericksburg and then the speeding trucks on the 10, and now the open highway without any fear except that which filled her about Jace.

The sun was still high, though evening was coming on. Not much traffic out here now. Deni opened the bike up all the way, the high-powered machine taking her swiftly down the road.

Shifters weren't allowed to buy new vehicles, but Deni always thought Harleys were better once they were broken in. Ellison had tinkered with this one until it purred like a lion, or maybe a snow leopard.

Deni ran it so fast she almost missed the 55, which jogged from this road west and a little north. She sped down it, squinting against the bright sun, nice and hot still in late July.

The 55 ended in a T junction with the 277, one leg of the T going north, the other going south. Deni stopped at a little pulloff at the crossroads and looked around. One truck rumbled past south, and a car sped north, its headlights turned on against the gathering twilight. No road went west from here except for a dirt track that headed off into the wilderness.

But Ronan had said they were *west* of this intersection, and so that was where they were.

Deni waited until the road was clear, then she glided the bike across the highway and onto the faint dirt path that led into nothing. Her wolf senses kicked in as she rode. She'd taken off her helmet at the crossroads, and now she could see, hear, and smell as a Shifter while her human body navigated the bike.

As the sky darkened, the huge arch of it brushed with stars, Deni saw a tiny orange light far to her left. The narrow dirt road bent to her right, taking her away from it, and she had no way of knowing whether the track would curve around again to where she wanted to go.

Deni shut off the bike, stripped off her clothes, stretched her limbs, and changed to her wolf.

Once in wolf form, she smelled the greasy smoke from faraway burning fuel, the scent making her gag. Deni trotted into the empty land, homing in on the fire.

She passed oil wells, stark metal giants against the twilit sky, their heads moving up and down, clanking as they pumped. But they were insignificant, an affectation of humans. Deni was wolf now, nothing more, and the night flowed to her.

After a long time of unceasing trotting, she made it to what she now saw was the smoldering wreck of a small airplane. Inside the perimeter of the fire's light, she saw the hulking forms of Ronan and Tiger and the tall one of Spike bending over a heap on the ground.

Jace? Deni's heart pounded as she sped up. No, Deni saw and scented as she neared the others. The man on the ground was human, probably the pilot, Marlo. She smelled no stench of death, so Marlo was still alive. Ronan and Spike were lashing him onto a stretcher, preparing to load him into a pickup that was parked nearby.

Tiger saw her and gave her a long look then he turned back to helping with Marlo.

Another wolf ran out of the darkness and straight to Deni—Ellison, large and gray, his wolf's eyes meeting hers. Ellison showed sorrow but also anger.

What the hell are you doing here? his body language said. *What part of 'don't you dare come out here' didn't you understand?*

Where's Jace? Deni snapped back, stopping herself from throwing herself at him and howling in anguish.

Don't know. Lost his scent.

Deni growled and rushed past him. She heard Ellison snarl a curse behind her and follow.

Deni dashed into the firelight, earning a startled look

from the Shifters there. Sean, sword on his back, started to step in front of her, but Deni ran around him to Tiger.

You're supposed to be so good at search and rescue, she growled up at Tiger. *Where is he?*

Deni glared at him, willing him to understand, but she was a wolf, and he a tiger, and who knew what got through?

Tiger watched her, his brows furrowed over his golden eyes. "You have to find him," he said.

Why haven't you?

Tiger kept staring at her. "*You* have to."

"Tiger, a little help here," Ronan called to him.

Tiger locked gazes with Deni a beat longer then he turned away to where Ronan was doing something near the burning debris, Deni had no idea what.

Deni growled in frustration and ran from the firelight, searching the perimeter of the crash site for Jace's scent.

She picked it up a little way beyond the wreck, when the wind blew the smoke from her face—Jace, loud and clear. She started off after him.

Already tried that, came Ellison's growl. *Lost it pretty quick.*

Deni wasn't listening. Each species of Shifter had an advantage over the others. Felines could see brilliantly in the dark, and they were *fast*. Bears had great strength and also stamina, probably because they slept so much, Deni had always privately thought.

But wolves beat both bears and Felines in the ability to follow scent. No Shifter could outdo a Lupine on a scent trail.

A wolf's second prowess was communication. Wolves

howled from hill to hill, passing information, warning, claiming territory. Their nonverbal skills were the best of any Shifter.

Right now, Deni needed only scent. Let Ellison howl at her—she had a mate to find.

She lost Jace's trail fairly soon, as Ellison had warned her, near another oil well, this one capped. The metallic stench of old oil and rusting machinery cancelled out the warmer scent of Shifter, and Deni sat down on her haunches, bereft.

Jace had come this way, though, that was certain. Whether he'd doubled back, or was lying hurt somewhere, Deni couldn't tell.

But Jace was her *mate*. They shared the mate bond— no doubt about it. Deni felt it inside her, its warmth around her heart, filling her with strength.

Deni's accident had robbed her of most of her confidence. She'd gone through episodes where she'd forgotten who she was and didn't know anyone around her—she'd attacked Ellison, and she'd turned on her friends and sometimes her own cubs.

Terrified of hurting those she loved, she'd locked herself into a tiny world, where she went out little, and kept herself from fighting, or even enjoying herself too much.

She'd not been able to ride a motorcycle, even behind someone else, as she'd explained to Jace, after she'd been run down, growing terrified even at the thought. Seeing the dangerous man who'd hurt her die had helped her begin to find closure, but the lingering fears died hard.

The loss of control—the feral rising up in her and

taking over—bothered her the most. But in this place, in the darkness, Deni realized that the only way she would find her mate would be to surrender to the beast inside her.

She moved away from the oil well, then sat down and closed her eyes. Deni drew long breaths, scenting past the barrier of the oil and the fire, searching the night.

She remembered what had gone through her when she'd seen Broderick attack Jace at the fight club. She hadn't known Jace was her mate then, but something in Deni had made her attack Broderick, to fight alongside Jace and protect him.

Deni brought to life the rage that had washed over her then, remembering the feel and taste of it. She let go of all rational thought and let the beast come.

Her Collar sparked once, but her coherence left her, and instinct took over.

The wolf put her head down and sniffed the ground, walking at first, then moving faster. She crisscrossed back and forth over open earth and then down a rocky wash.

She found nothing, but Deni's wolf wouldn't let her grow frustrated. Tracking by scent took patience and time.

She climbed up the other side of the wash, continuing to hunt, covering every inch of ground she could. She moved farther and farther from the wreck, leaving the other Shifters far behind. Still she found nothing. Either Jace had left some other way than his own feet, or he'd hidden himself well.

Deni sat down in the darkness, hearing the slither of snakes in the dried grass, they giving her a wide berth. She could scent nothing but the night now—the grains of dust on the wind, the coolness of water far away, the wild dryness of Texas, unchanged for centuries. No wild-cats, except those at the wreck behind her, no Shifters at all.

Maybe scent wasn't what she should be following, the dim thought came. Deni contemplated that in her quiet wolf way, then she closed her eyes, wrapped herself around the mate bond, and sent it outward.

There. An answering tug, far to the west and south of where she stood. Jace was there. False scents could be laid, and scents could be covered, but nothing could disguise the almost painful tug of the mate bond.

Deni loped back the way she'd come, across the wash, and started running, drawn to Jace with surety.

She heard Ellison howl in frustration somewhere behind her. He'd lost her scent and couldn't find her in the darkness. No matter. Deni would find her mate and bring him home, and all would be well.

———

Jace sensed her coming. The snow leopard stopped in midrun, pulled up short as though someone had snapped a tether on him and yanked him to a halt.

He'd been running, putting as much distance between himself and the wreck as he possibly could. Whoever found him—Shifter or human—would want to drag him back to captivity, Collars, and rules. Shifters taming them-selves, Jace was realizing, didn't mean safety. It meant submission.

But his mate was coming.

Jace stopped on a little rise, a rare thing in this flat

world. He sat down, panting, wrapping his cat tail around him as he waited for her.

Deni raced out of the dry grasses, her body a streak of gray under the moonlight. She came fast, running up the rise, not stopping. She let out a joyful yip and barreled into Jace so hard they rolled together down the other side of the little hill and ended up in a heap on the bottom.

Deni shifted into her human form, naked, her body outlined by starlight. Tears streaked her face.

"I found you." She wrapped her arms around Jace's leopard, who huffed and nuzzled her. "I found you."

Jace licked her face, tasting her tears, and Deni laughed as his rough tongue nearly pushed her over.

Come with me, my love, Jace urged. *Into the wild, where we belong.*

Deni pulled back, studying him. "Are you all right? It looks like they're taking Marlo to a hospital. You should get looked at too."

For answer, Jace jumped on her, knocking her to the ground. Deni's mouth curved to laughter as she held an armful of fur.

"Seriously, Jace. I was worried about you. Everyone is. I thought you were dead."

The tears returned. Jace licked them away again, this time being gentle.

"I was so scared for you that I jumped on my motorcycle and rode away without realizing it. Did you hear me? I rode. *My motorcycle.* By myself. And I wasn't afraid!"

Jace licked her again. *I'm glad, my heart. You are healing.*

"Ride back with me. That will be even better."

Nope. Not going back.

"Jace." Deni stroked his head, and Jace wanted to purr. "I don't speak Feline very well. Change and talk to me."

Jace didn't want to change. He'd stay cat, she'd stay wolf, and they'd make a den somewhere. They were smart enough to hunt and evade hunters, and to teach their cubs to do the same. He loved her scent, which was stirring his mating frenzy.

"What's wrong?" Deni asked him, stroking him again. "I let go of my biggest fear just now—losing control of myself—to let my wolf take over so I could find you. And you know what? I'm fine. Look." She spread her arms. "I didn't go feral. I found you, and I didn't lose myself. I don't have to be afraid anymore." She held Jace again, his mate strong and warm. "The crash must have been horrible. But don't lose yourself, Jace. Please. Come back to me."

There was nothing wrong with Jace. He was free, and Collarless. But it was dark and Deni hadn't touched his neck. She didn't understand yet.

"Please, Jace. I need you."

Tears trickled from her eyes again, tugging Jace out of his animal focus. He shifted, not as smoothly as he usually did, but jerking and groaning with the pain of it. His cat did *not* want to let go.

"It came off," Jace said, the words bearing a Feline growl. "Look. The Collar. Gone."

He took Deni's hand and put it to his neck.

Deni's eyes widened. She brushed Jace's bare neck, which didn't hurt at all, skimming her fingers around to his throat. "What happened?"

"Don't know. Was out of the wreck before I realized.

Maybe the fire. Maybe it takes intense heat to melt them off."

Jace touched Deni's face, his need for her kicking him hard. Deni moved to his touch, then she grabbed his hand and stared at it. "What is *that?*"

Jace glanced at his palm. It still hurt, and now he saw why. His palm was burned but crossed by a gold streak, which he realized was Deni's bracelet. The slender gold band had been fused into his skin.

CHAPTER THIRTEEN

"Hurts," Jace said. And *itched* too.

Deni kissed his palm, her lips cool. "I can see that. What happened?"

"It must have heated and melted," Jace said. "Sorry, Den. I promised I'd bring it back to you."

"You did." Deni touched his face and gave him a smile that tightened the bond around his heart. "Let's go home."

"We are home." Deni was under him, her body soft, her scent and warmth making him forget pain. "Stay here with me."

She looked worried again. "We need to go back. You have friends and family who love you, and they're afraid for you."

Jace nuzzled her. "But I'm free of everything. I'm done with being used, hurt, experimented on. I'm finished being easygoing Jace, in the background. I have my mate, my life. I have *you*."

Deni's expression softened. "Yes."

The mating frenzy was kicking in with her too; Jace saw it in her eyes. Her fingers were hot as she brushed his face, finding his hurts.

The touch of the mate healed. Jace closed his eyes and knew his wounds were closing, his burns easing, his Shifter metabolism helped by the gentle caress of his true mate.

"Jace, stay with me."

Jace opened his eyes, realizing he'd started to revert to his leopard. He forced himself into human shape again. He needed to stay human right now, because he wanted to have her.

He growled low in his throat. Deni recognized the sound, her eyes becoming darker, filled with need. She ran her hands up his back and to his neck.

Jace knew that once he started kissing her, he'd not be able to stop, and he didn't care. He slanted his mouth over hers, tasting her heat, her frenzy. It built and grew, calling to his own frenzy, which answered.

The kisses turned fierce. Jace bit down on Deni's lower lip, eliciting a gasp from her but also laughter. She arched against him while she laughed, her body moving in wonderful ways.

Jace held her down with a strong hand and entered her. As he slid inside, his world changed.

The selfish wildness that had infused him when he'd realized he'd lost the Collar whirled into one tight focus.

Deni. She alone mattered.

Jace wanted to be with her—forever—and nowhere else. Even if he had to return to Shiftertown with her, to still be a captive, it didn't matter anymore. Jace would find a way to be with her, he vowed this. And with Deni, he'd always be free.

He fit into her as though she'd been made for him. Jace kissed her lips, her face, her lips again as he drew back then stroked inside her even deeper.

Deni sucked in her breath and then she smiled, her eyes darkening in pleasure. She touched his cheek as she liked to, her fingertips a soft counterpart to the crazed need inside him.

Jace rocked into her, her body squeezing down on him and turning him wild. Raw need flooded him, relieved only by the wonderful feeling of thrusting into her. Stroke after stroke, loving her, cradling her body with one arm so the hard dirt wouldn't cut into her.

"My mate," he whispered. "I saw you, and never wanted to be without you."

Deni shook her head, fingers threading through his hair. "Jace."

"Be mine," Jace said. "Say it. Always mine."

Deni smiled. "*Mine.*"

He returned the smile, his fierce. "Forever."

"Yes."

The word turned into a groan. Deni's grip bit into his shoulders, and she held him while she shuddered and cried his name, her thrusts meeting his. Jace bent his head and nipped her neck, tasting the metallic tang of her Collar.

He'd have it off her—he'd figure out how. And she'd be free, with him. The pain would be gone, and Deni would heal. He'd be with her, next to her, helping her all the way.

"*Jace.*"

Deni's groan filled him with frenzy. His thrusts grew

faster, his growls deeper. He'd go to ground with her, and they'd do this all day long and into the night. She'd smile at him, beautiful and sensual, and wrap her arms around him, wanting to do it again.

"Dani. *Goddess.*" Jace lost his seed into her, pumping his hips while she laughed to the stars.

Jace raised his head, his body slick with sweat, and kissed her lips, her mouth hot with afterglow. "I love you," he said, his heart in every word.

"I love you too, Jace. Always my mate."

Jace was still hard, pulsing with need for her. He gave her a feral smile as he thrust into her again, beginning the rhythm once more.

Deni gave him a startled look, and then she laughed. The laughter soon turned to groans, and they gave themselves over to the frenzy, their cries ringing against the millions of bright stars.

———

Ellison found Jace and Deni where they lay together in the warm night.

Of course he did—Deni knew they'd given him plenty of time to find their scent, and they must have been throwing off pheromones like crazy, providing an easy trail to follow.

Ellison came trotting up as his wolf, then shifted to human and groaned. "Not *again.* I swear, I can't come near you two without finding you tangled together." His voice held relief though, even rejoicing.

Jace helped Deni to her feet and put her behind his

warm body, but when he faced Ellison, he wasn't defensive and angry. He showed his open hands, a posture of peace.

"Congratulate us, Ellison," Jace rumbled. "I'm mate-claiming your sister, Deni Rowe, under the light of the moon, the Goddess, and in front of a witness—you. I plan to ask Liam or my dad to perform the mating rituals as soon as they can."

Ellison stopped, moonlight gleaming on his light hair and wolf-gray eyes. He was the leader of Deni's small pack, but answering the mate-claim was Deni's choice.

"You good with that, Den?" Ellison asked, his voice going soft.

"Yeah." Deni slid her arms around Jace from behind, loving the tall solidness of his body, his warm scent, the feel of his skin as she kissed his shoulder. "I'm good with that. I accept the mate-claim. Jace?" She heard the shaking in her voice. "You ready to go home? To my home I mean— it's closer right now. We can call your dad from there. I be he's worried sick."

Deni held her breath, waiting for Jace to want to return to the leopard, to insist Deni come with him into the wild, or leave on his own if she wouldn't. He wore no Collar now —there was nothing to stop him.

Even so, life in the wild was dangerous. Jace could be found, hunted, killed. And he could still go feral—Shifters who lived on their own, letting their beasts take over, often did go feral.

The Shifters Ellison's mate, Maria, had been rescued from had refused to take Collars, hidden out, and become feral and cruel. Collars, for their pain, and the Shifter laws, for their restrictions, at least worked to help keep Shifters sane.

Jace turned in Deni's arms and looked down at her, his face in shadow. Ellison waited behind him, tense, uncertain.

Deni's heart ached, both with the bond and with worry. Jace looked better, his burns pale streaks in the moonlight. He looked stronger too, and more at ease, any uncertainty he might have felt for his place in the world gone.

Then he smiled. Every bit of love was in the smile, every bit of tenderness. He brushed back a lock of Deni's hair, his fingers warm.

"We'll want to tell your cubs you accepted my mate-claim," Jace said. "So yeah. Let's go home."

———

A Shifter meeting was called in Liam's house the next day, after Jace and Deni had rested from the long drive back to Austin—well, Deni remembered with a blush —they'd done more than just rest. The meeting included Eric Warden, Jace's father.

Deni's heart squeezed as Eric strode across the house to meet Jace when he came in, father enfolding son in a long, hard embrace. Eric's mate, Iona, who was heavy with Eric's child, also hugged Jace, wiping away her tears when she released him.

Jace reached for Deni, who'd hung back from the family greeting, and pulled her forward. "You remember Deni Rowe, Ellison's sister."

Eric understood their connection as soon as he looked at Deni, and Iona caught on a second later. Eric gazed at Deni with eyes the same color as his son's, then he put his big arms around Deni and pulled her into an embrace equally as tight as the one he'd shared with Jace.

"Thank you, child," Eric said, his voice rumbling into her ear. "Welcome to the family."

He stood Deni back and studied her, a satisfied look in his eyes. Iona slid past Eric and hugged Deni herself.

"Congratulations, you two." Iona winked at Deni as she stepped away from her. "Jace is a sweetheart. A keeper."

Deni smiled her agreement. "I think so."

"And now Collar-free," Eric said. "Thank the Goddess."

Deni understood Eric was thanking the Goddess for more than Jace's Collar being off. A shudder went through Eric, which Deni recognized as a father's relief that his cub was safe and whole.

"Jace has a theory about that," Liam said from where he lounged on a window seat in the living room. He held his black-haired daughter in the curve of his arm, little Katriona watching the adults with interest. "Carry on, lad."

Jace held up his hand, which bore a red streak. Last night, when they'd returned to the Austin Shiftertown and after Sean and Dylan had gotten Marlo to a hospital—the resilient man was on the mend—Sean and Jace had painfully dug the remnants of the gold chain from Jace's hand. Andrea had quickly done a healing on him, then

Deni had completed the healing in the privacy of the Rowe family's secret basement.

"Fionn saw the bracelet last night when he was visiting Andrea," Jace said. "Andrea told me this morning that Fionn told her that this bracelet is made of Fae gold. Passed down through the female line of many generations of Deni's mother's family. Shifters used to live in Faerie—why couldn't one of them have had access to Fae gold?" Jace slid his arm around Deni. "I was holding the bracelet, which Deni gave me as a keepsake, when the plane went down. I went through hell, nearly burned alive. The heat must have melted it into me, where it entered my nervous system or bloodstream, or skin cells, or something. I haven't figured that part out. But somehow, my Collar loosened and fell away, without hurting me. Though maybe I didn't notice the pain while my fur was being fried off."

"The third element," Sean said. He dangled a Collar from his hand, Jace's Collar, which Sean had found in the wreckage. "Silver and human technology, fused together by Fae gold. Whether the gold is already in the Collar or only put into it when the Collar goes on the Shifter's neck, we don't know yet."

"Or how to use that knowledge to get the Collars off," Jace said.

Sean studied Jace's Collar, which looked remarkably intact for its time in the crucible the plane had become. "Maybe a syringe of the liquid gold carefully injected into the Shifter will loosen it? Or simply rubbed on the skin? Will be tricky, this, since Fae gold's pretty hard to find, according to Fionn. Fionn says he'll help us, but even he says it's very rare."

"He claims he has it in the walls in his house," Jace said. "Tell him to dig it out for us."

"He explained that to me," Sean said, without smiling. "He said when it was all chipped away it would only be an ounce or so. But we'll work on finding a source. And start trying out techniques. It might still be very painful."

Jace touched the fake Collar around his neck, put there courtesy of Liam and Dylan this morning. "Well, you can try it on someone not me. I'm done messing with Collars."

Sean nodded in understanding. "You've got it, lad. Volunteers only. But I'm thinking some will put up with a little hot gold on their skin to be free of these bloody devices."

"Me," Deni said. "You can try it first on me. Use whatever is left in the bracelet. I'm sure my mother would be fine with me using it to free myself and my mate."

Jace's hold on her tightened. "No. Not until they know what they're doing."

"Sean will figure it out." Deni leaned into Jace, feeling warm and protected. "I want this damned Collar off. I want to heal all the way. With you, and without the Collar."

Jace growled, but she saw sympathy in his eyes. "All right, but I'm with you every step of the way. Every second. And if Sean hurts you more than necessary, he answers to me."

"Oh, good," Sean said. "No pressure. Don't worry, lass. I'll be trying these ideas on meself as well. I have a mate who can make us all better if I screw up."

"I *hope* I can," Andrea said. She held her son close, his gray eyes so much like his mother's.

"I'm just feeling better about this all the time," Sean said.

"We can do volunteers from our Shiftertown too," Eric said. "Those who would most benefit. If there proves to be so little Fae gold, the weaker Shifters should be released first, those whose Collars hurt them the most. Those of us who can control the Collars' effects—we'll suck it up for a while."

"Speaking of your Shiftertown," Deni said, and Eric focused on her.

"Don't worry—I'll make sure Jace can move here officially," Eric said. "And have leave to visit me and bring you with him as often as possible." Eric swallowed, the light in his eyes dimming. "I'll miss him, but I know what a mate bond is like." His hand drifted to Iona's, and his mate rose on tiptoe and kissed his cheek.

Another thing Jace was doing for her, Deni reflected. Traditionally, Shifter women moved into the homes of their mates, leaving their own families behind.

But it would be difficult to obtain permission to move Deni *and* her two cubs to the Las Vegas Shiftertown, and it would also mean leaving Ellison. To prevent Deni having to leave her sons behind, Jace had volunteered to move here instead. A break with tradition, but a kind one.

"Well," Liam said, pushing himself from the window seat and handing Katriona to Kim. "I'm looking forward to conducting yet another mating ceremony. Unless Eric fights me for the honor. But we have other business at hand. Tiger."

Tiger unfolded his big arms and moved to the basement door—the door to the true basement, not the Morrisseys' secret space. The Shifters at this meeting were Liam and family and Liam's trackers, plus Eric and Iona. Liam had asked for Eric's advice on the sticky problem Deni had uncovered at the Shifter bar.

Tiger unlocked and opened the door to reveal the young woman Deni had caught with the phone that showed she'd made many calls to the police.

She'd washed off the Shifter groupie makeup but stared around at the Shifters with defiance in her eyes. Broderick, who'd insisted on guarding her, brought her up the last of the stairs with his hand lightly on her shoulder. Broderick's gray eyes swept the trackers, and he looked almost as defiant as the young woman.

"This is Joanne Greene," Liam said. "She's been following Shifters around and reporting things to the police—the fight club, what Shifters do at the bar—and asking the cops to talk to Shifters and watch them."

Deni had wondered what Liam would do with the young woman. Dylan now went to her, and the woman's defiance dissolved into terror. Dylan stopped a foot in front of her, in her personal space.

"Tell my son what you told me," Dylan said.

Her chin came up. "Why should I?"

She was young, even for a human. In her midtwenties, Deni guessed, if that.

Connor, who was only a little younger than Joanne, shook his head. "I'd tell him. If you think Grandda's scary, wait 'til you face Uncle Liam."

Broderick squeezed her shoulder. "Best get it over with." He sounded sympathetic, interestingly enough.

Joanne took a deep breath. "Because you took my sister," she said.

Liam blinked in surprise, and so did most of the Shifters present. "Your sister?"

"My sister, Nancy," Joanne said. "She's the true Shifter groupie. Loves to chase Shifters. She was here, in Shiftertown. Then she disappeared. What did you do with her?"

Liam gave her a blank look. "We didn't do anything with her, lass. Where was she last? With what Shifter?"

"I don't know." Joanne's eyes flashed anger. "Does it matter what Shifter? She was at your bar, then she went to your fight club. That was a few weeks ago. She hasn't come home since."

"And the human police agree with you that a Shifter must have taken her?" Deni couldn't help asking.

Joanne looked even angrier. "They say they have no evidence of harm. They think she ran off on her own."

Dylan didn't move any closer to Joanne, but his look of menace was hard. "And so you stir up trouble for all Shifters, endangering us, our mates, our cubs, without coming to us and asking about her first?"

Joanne stepped back in fear, bumping into Broderick, but she spoke in a clear voice.

"Come to you? Why should I come to *you*?"

Dylan started to answer, but Broderick took a step sideways, putting himself in a position where he could defend Joanne against the others if need be.

"Go easy on her," he said to Dylan. "She's afraid for her sister. Don't tell me you wouldn't do the same thing if you lost track of someone you loved inside another Shiftertown."

Dylan's expression hardened. "No, what I would do is find the right culprit and shake him until he coughed up what he knew. And *then* decide whether to let him live."

"She's been telling me about it," Broderick said, as Joanne gazed at Dylan in fear. "I don't think a Shifter took her sister, but it looks like *something* happened around a Shifter event. You and Liam have all kinds of resources. Help her."

Liam gave Broderick a thoughtful look. "Maybe we will. Dad."

Dylan looked over Broderick and Joanne, then he turned away.

Without a word, he walked out of the living room and then out the front door with an even stride. The bang of the door in his wake was loud, and for a moment, no one said anything.

Dylan often did such things—keeping his own council and walking away to solve problems on his own. He was older than most Shifters in Shiftertown, and had experience and wisdom no one else had. The Shifters had learned to tolerate his abruptness.

Liam cleared his throat. "Since you like her so much, Broderick, you're in charge of her," he said. "I don't want her talking to the police, or going anywhere or doing anything without me knowing. Got it?"

"Sure," Broderick said. "Lighten up, Liam."

Liam blinked again. Deni saw Liam deliberately let Broderick's admonition go before he gave Joanne a slow nod.

"We're going to help you find out what happened to your sister. But you behave—understand?"

Joanne was bewildered—she must have thought the Shifters would kill her, or at least imprison her and do terrible things to her—but she nodded. Broderick stayed protectively in front of her, and Liam ended the meeting.

"I think he's smitten," Deni said to Jace as they walked back to her house across the street. "Broderick, I mean."

They mounted the porch steps of Deni's house, and Jace pushed Deni against a porch post. "So am I. Smitten is a good word for it."

His kiss stirred fires that hadn't gone out. Deni wound her arms around his neck and enjoyed him for a moment.

"I meant what I said," she murmured as their mouths drew apart. "About the Collar. I'll let Sean do what he needs to. I want it off."

"I do too." Jace touched the chain on her neck. "I'll be with you, Den. And when you're free, we'll do some celebrating."

"Why wait?" Deni smiled into his face, and Jace's serious look dissolved into a wicked grin.

"Wild woman," Jace said.

"Always."

Jace led her into the empty house and to the basement, the two of them laughing as they stumbled down the stairs. Jace kicked the door closed at the bottom as he kissed her again.

They waltzed their way into the bedroom they'd been using, hands stripping off each other's clothes while their mouths locked into long, hot kisses.

"I love you, Jace Warden," Deni said as they went down onto the bed.

"I love you too, Deni Rowe. So much." Jace drew her

up to him, stoking the fires inside her. "Thank you for finding me."

"You found *me*," Deni said. "Healed me too."

"Mmm." Jace closed his eyes as he slid inside her. His voice went low. "You healed me. We healed each other." He put his hand on hers, the streak where the bracelet had burned him already closed to a red scar. Their fingers touched, spread. "You and me. One."

Jace laced his fingers through hers, and Deni closed their hands together. "One," she said, then she let out a cry as Jace thrust into her with a firmer stroke. "Always."

"Always," Jace said, and then there was nothing but the sounds of lovemaking, and happiness.

Sorrow fled, and Deni proved to herself what a beautiful thing it was losing control in the arms of the Shifter she loved.

EPILOGUE

D eni and Jace were mated in the full-sun ceremony the next day, bringing the blessings of the Father God on the union. The full-moon ceremony, the final sealing of the mates, happened a few nights later, after Deni had had her Collar removed, at her insistence.

It was severely painful, and how Sean got the remaining gold from the bracelet to blend with the Collar and loosen it, Deni wasn't quite sure.

She only knew that the Collar had come off, link by slow link. It had hurt, yes, but Deni knew her release had come with nowhere near the agony that had suffused Jace when they'd tried to take his Collar off him. She'd also not felt the need to shift to her beast to give in to her feral instincts, as Jace had. The Fae gold made the difference.

Jace had been there, right next to her, snarling at a nervous Sean every minute. When Sean had lifted the Collar free and Deni took a long breath, Jace had pulled her hard into his arms, his eyes wet.

Deni, now fitted with a fake silver Collar, stood with Jace in the grove behind the houses under the moonlight, with Eric and Liam in front of them. Both had decided they'd jointly perform the full-moon ceremony—Liam because it was his Shiftertown and he was fond of Deni, Eric because Jace was his son.

Shifters gathered in circles, the chanting already beginning. So was the drinking and partying. Ellison stood next to Deni, proud and grinning, Maria on his arm smiling her sweet smile. Behind Deni were Jackson and Will, deliriously happy for their mother but plenty willing to tease both her and Jace.

Iona had come, standing next to Eric, with Eric's sister, Cassidy, and her mate, a human named Diego, next to her. Marlo, recovered from his bang-up but lamenting about the loss of his beloved plane, had also come.

So had the young woman called Joanne, who was being looked after by Broderick and his brothers. She'd relaxed a bit around Shifters, at least around Broderick's gruff family. She was still worried about her sister, but Dylan already had things in motion. They'd find her.

As the moon rose, its cool light flooding the clearing, Liam held up his hands for silence. He and Eric stepped forward, Eric smiling in his warm way.

"By the light of the Mother Goddess," Liam began.

"I acknowledge this mating," Eric finished. "The blessings of the Goddess go with you, Son." He put his arms around Jace. "And Daughter." Eric turned and embraced Deni, Jace's hand on Deni's back as she hugged Eric in return.

And then there was laughter, many more hugs, with

Deni almost squashed by the enthusiastic ones her sons gave her. Ronan's giant bear hug competed with Will's and Jackson's for force. Tiger even hugged her, then gave her a nod, as though satisfied she'd finally wised up and done the right thing, bringing Jace home.

Shifters whooped, howled, screamed. The mating ceremony was a fertility feast, and Shiftertown would be fertile tonight.

Deni hadn't felt the dizziness or beginnings of nausea that had triggered her episodes of near-madness since Jace had been brought home safely to Shiftertown. She'd made a breakthrough, she thought, out in the wild, choosing to give in to her instincts, which had helped her find her mate.

The fact that she'd been able to pull herself out of the instinctive state once she'd found Jace, and hadn't gone insane, had restored some of her confidence. The mate bond also helped erase her fear, and so had the removal of the Collar.

Deni didn't know exactly when she'd been healed, but she knew the process had begun when she'd met Jace that night at the fight club.

Music poured into the night. Deni danced with her sons, then Ellison, Liam, and Eric, with a circle of girls—Andrea, Kim, Iona, Glory, Elizabeth, Myka, Carly. The cubs ran around, undisciplined, shouting and screaming in their own games.

Finally, Deni ended up with Jace again. He tugged her close, his eyes going pale green with barely contained mating frenzy.

"Remember how this started?" he asked.

"You getting your ass kicked?" Deni answered, laughing.

"Me *saving* your ass," Jace said. "And then having it."

"Don't you wish.'"

"I do." Jace leaned close. "I wanted you again and again, Deni. I went through a lot to keep you by my side, didn't I?"

Deni nodded. "I'm glad you did."

Jace kissed her again, his smiles gone. "It's dark out here tonight. No one would miss us."

She gave him a teasing smile. "Maybe we should be more civilized about it, now that we're mated."

"Screw that." Jace's hold tightened, his hand warming the small of her back. "I like being wild with you, Den. My heart."

"Mmm." Deni kissed him, then wrenched herself out of his arms. "Let's be wild, then." She took the garland from her head and threw it, spinning, away from her. Shifter women shouted laughter and scrambled after it.

"Catch me if you can, Feline," Deni said to Jace, and she swung away, dashing into the night.

She heard a growl of frustrated wildcat, then another one of determination.

Deni ran, but she knew she'd never outdistance a leopard who'd do anything to bring down his prey. She did try, though, so Jace would have a challenge.

But when his strong arms came around her in the darkness beyond the bonfires, Jace's kisses frantically falling on her flesh, Deni knew she'd never been so happy to be caught.

Shifters Unbound

Pride Mates

Primal Bonds

Bodyguard

Wild Cat

Hard Mated

Mate Claimed

"Perfect Mate" (novella)

Lone Wolf

Tiger Magic

Feral Heat

Wild Wolf

Bear Attraction

Mate Bond

Lion Eyes

Bad Wolf

Wild Things

White Tiger

Guardian's Mate

Red Wolf

Midnight Wolf

Tiger Striped

A Shifter Christmas Carol

Iron Master

The Last Warrior

Tiger's Daughter

Bear Facts

Stray Cat

Shifter Made ("Prequel" novella)

Stormwalker Series (w/a Allyson James)

Stormwalker

Firewalker

Shadow Walker

"Double Hexed"

Nightwalker

Dreamwalker

Dragon Bites

Wing Dancer

Shape Changer

(novella featuring Dylan)
The Last Warrior (Ben and Rhianne)
(Ben crosses over to other Shiftertowns)
Tiger's Daughter (Connor and Tiger-Girl)

Kendrick's Group

(Most cross over with Austin Shifters)
Lion Eyes (Seamus and Bree)
White Tiger (Kendrick and Addison)
Red Wolf (Jaycee and Dimitri)

Las Vegas Shifters

Wild Cat (Cassidy and Diego)
Mate Claimed (Eric and Iona)
Perfect Mate (Nell and Cormac)
Wild Wolf (Graham and Misty)
Iron Master (Stuart Reid and Peigi)
Bear Facts (Shane and Freya)
Stray Cat (Xav and Lindsay)

North Carolina Shifters

Mate Bond (Bowman and Kenzie.
Crossover with Las Vegas Shifters)

New Orleans Shifters

Midnight Wolf (Angus and Tamsin.
Crosses over with Austin Shifters and Zander)

Montana Shifters

Guardian's Mate (Zander and Rae)

Note: I include Zander with the Montana Shifters, because Rae is from the Montana Shiftertown, but Zander moves between all the groups. It's his way.

Check my website:

https://www.jenniferashley.com

for additions as I continue to explore all the Shiftertowns!

All my best,

Jennifer Ashley

New York Times bestselling and award-winning author Jennifer Ashley has more than 120 published novels and novellas in mystery, romance, historical fiction, and urban fantasy under the names Jennifer Ashley, Allyson James, and Ashley Gardner. Jennifer's books have been translated into more than a dozen languages and have earned starred reviews in *Publisher's Weekly* and *Booklist*. When she isn't writing, Jennifer enjoys playing music (guitar, piano, flute), reading, hiking, cooking, and building dollhouse miniatures.

More about Jennifer's books can be found at
http://www.jenniferashley.com

To keep up to date on her new releases, join her newsletter here:
http://eepurl.com/47kLL